'The beggarly question of parentage — what is it, after all? What does it matter, when you come to think of it, whether a child is yours by blood or not? All the little ones of our time are collectively the children of us adults of the time, and entitled to our general care. That excessive regard of parents for their own children, and their dislike of other people's, is, like class-feeling . . . a mean exclusiveness at bottom.'

Thomas Hardy
Jude the Obscure
1894

Margaret Sutherland is a New Zealand writer who has lived in Australia since 1986. She has published several novels and collections of short stories, has held the New Zealand Scholarship in Letters and has received two Australia Council writing fellowships. Her work has been included in many anthologies. For further details, visit Margaret's website at: www.margaretsutherland.com

WINDSONG

Australia. Martin Ainsworth, a disgraced English teacher, escapes back to his home in the city of Armidale, hoping to recover, with memories of youthful love and ambition. But Annie Marshall, his first love, turns up and the past is anything but dead. Meanwhile, Martin's ex-wife hands over the fulltime care of his teenage son. Confused, Martin turns to Sara, the owner of his apartment, and attempts to steer a course between love and duty. And while Sara and Annie confront their own decisions, the children become innocent participants in the break-ups and regroupings of modern family life and love.

Books by Margaret Sutherland
Published by The House of Ulverscroft:

LEAVING GAZA

MARGARET SUTHERLAND

WINDSONG

Complete and Unabridged

ULVERSCROFT
Leicester

First published in Great Britain in 2008 by

First Large Print Edition
published 2009

British Library CIP Data

Sutherland, Margaret.
  Windsong
  1. Teachers- -Fiction. 2. First loves- -Fiction.
  3. Children of divorced parents- -Fiction.
  4. Fathers and sons- -Fiction. 5. Australia- -Fiction.
  6. Large type books.
  I. Title
  823.9′14–dc22

  ISBN 978–1–84782–786–9

Published by
F. A. Thorpe (Publishing)
Anstey, Leicestershire
Set by Words & Graphics Ltd.
Anstey, Leicestershire
Printed and bound in Great Britain by
T. J. International Ltd., Padstow, Cornwall

This book is printed on acid-free paper

1

Martin

I stand by the old lemon tree, watching the boys kick a football around. Suddenly the ball takes an unexpected arc and veers towards me. I manage to angle it back to the group and Adam gives a shout of approval. *Good one, Dad!* My son has certainly come a long way from that sullen boy I met at Armidale railway station last year. At that time I could hardly bear the prospect of putting up with him for the school holidays. Now his praise delights me. I feel a surge of pride and love for him. But then, so much has changed. More than I could ever have thought possible. Particularly given my state of mind a year ago. My life was at its lowest ebb. I'd taken long service leave and retreated to Armidale. Holiday or escape, does it matter? I came back to this town to reconsider my life. My drinking lapses had wiped reassuring definitions off the blackboard. The police had stopped me at 2 am as I drove along Hunter Street on the wrong side of the road. On weaving my way from the nightclub, it seems I turned right instead of left. Fortunately there was no oncoming traffic at the time. The officer who pursued me breathalysed me and ordered me into the paddy wagon. I was contained overnight in a cell. In due course the magistrate fined me $1200, revoked my license for six months and told me a man in my position should think most seriously about his actions. I agreed. My accustomed detachment was no help at all in this situation. This weak-willed fellow standing before the law was irresponsible, stupid and a danger to society. I had no respect for him.

Suddenly I understood why people sometimes turn their backs on family and career and disappear. Oh, I don't mean suicide. I just needed to get away and think. I confessed to my headmaster, a decent man who allowed human nature its down side. I outlined the facts and admitted my behaviour had been appalling.

'It's a pity, Martin. There were promotions under consideration.'

He didn't need to spell it out. I looked away, through his window where the cathedral was framed against an autumn sky.

'You've long service leave, haven't you?'

I nodded. 'Six months. Wouldn't that disrupt the curriculum?' Of course I hoped I was indispensable.

The headmaster didn't think so. 'This is a coincidence. You remember Peter Barnett?'

I scanned the page he handed me. It was an application from the English teacher who'd previously held my post. He was back from a three-year stint in America and sought a relieving position.

'Six months. That should work. Just about see the year out.'

He sat waiting while my gaze was drawn again to the window. That soaring spire filled me with loss that clenched my gut. I swallowed an awful sadness. My voice sounded thick when I answered him.

'Yes. I heard Peter was back.'

'He evidently wants a job. Might even have brought back some fresh ideas.' He'd chastised enough schoolboys to know the right place for the lecture. 'Martin, I know you're a dedicated teacher. You get good results and the boys like you. But you're wise to step back and take a good look at things. Pull your life into shape. I'll approve the leave. Shall we get on with the paperwork?'

He didn't say he'd be glad to see the back of me, but the school had an image to uphold and parents read court reports. So that was that.

Also in trouble, a small boy lurked outside

the door. I almost knocked him down. 'S-sorry, sir,' he stuttered.

'My fault,' I assured him. 'Headmaster's ready to see you.'

His timid smile faded and I touched his shoulder with the sympathy of conspirators. The stairs bore the wear and tear of a million shoes. Institutional smells of ripe fruit, wax polish and damp paper wafted in the corridor. A bell shrilled, followed by the scrape of chairs and the press of eager feet. I no longer had a place in this life I took for granted and frequently complained about. The Renaissance man self-image — teacher, composer, philosopher — lay in the dust. I had classes after recess. For now I had to get away. Ignoring the throng of boys I went quickly to the exit.

It was settled by Friday. Peter was keen to start immediately. I could meet him the following week and, after suitable briefing, be free. Colleagues on leave frequently set off to visit the Greek Isles or Europe. No hope of that! Apart from the justifiable fine I had to pay, my perennial financial problems ruled out travel. I decided on Armidale, where I'd gained my degree and met Annie. That love affair ended when I moved to Sydney. Annie stayed put. I heard she'd married almost at once and soon had a baby. We didn't keep in touch. Sometimes I'd think of her, living her domestic life in that high altitude while I rummaged in the morass of Sydney bars and dives. Maudlin on whisky and lack of sleep, I'd think *Annie, you had a lucky escape.* In those days I fancied I was the '80's answer to Bob Dylan. And I did have my moments when I gathered my audience in my hands. But most of the next years were lost in moving, marrying, and staring at two strangers, my wife and my wailing baby son. It was presumed I would change light bulbs and push a lawnmower. Fights, recriminations, tears. Divorce. I was shattered — by my own failure to honour vows, as much as by the loss of Carol and Adam.

Of course there have been women since; interesting liaisons, but I've ensured nothing's turned too serious. I set aside artistic dreams and settled for life as a teacher in a provincial city. No more trouble. No more binges. I've inherited my father's weakness for drink. He was that perennial fraud: a man who kept up appearances while spending his worst nature on wife and family. Compared to his temper and abuse, my lapses qualified as mere peccadilloes until the reality of a cell and a magistrate put paid to that delusion.

It was time to move on. My plans fell into place. I gave Peter a rundown on the curriculum. It happened that he was looking for accommodation and agreed to sub-let my unit, fully furnished even down to my cat, Seiko. Essentials I packed into a couple of suitcases. I booked a train ticket. The day before I was due to travel north, I took a last stroll through Newcastle town. Armidale was an inland city; I would miss these glimpses of ocean visible beyond the high-fenced railway lines. I stopped in at Pepperinas for a decent coffee and quick book browse. The thought of calling in to the school crossed my mind, but approaching the gates I changed my mind. Farewells had been said. I didn't belong there now. Instead I crossed the road to the cathedral and took a back pew, grateful for the respite. I'm not a believer but I do respect tradition. I sat a while, distracted by a fluttering above my head. My course was as astray as the sparrow vainly circling the vault of an illusory heaven.

★　★　★

I'd neglected one thing. Back at the unit I phoned my ex-wife, Carol, who lived in Sydney with her partner, Liz, and our son. Omitting the business with the police, I let her know my plans.

'You haven't forgotten you're having Adam

for the holidays? I'll be away.' Her business-like tone of voice made it plain she didn't want a twelve-year-old in tow. I said I didn't know where I'd be staying. We'd have to work something out.

'Make sure you do.' She wasn't happy.

'How's Adam?' I felt guilty even asking the question. Did I want an honest answer? My son and I were poles apart. He was a boy who'd been in trouble from day one, when I first set eyes on him, bruised and battered, deep indentations on his head where the forceps had dragged him from his mother. If Adam never visited me I didn't believe I'd mind. Our access visits were time-dragging affairs and we parted with a sense of jovial relief.

'I should tell you,' Carol was saying, 'he's been in with a bad set of kids. There was trouble recently. Shoplifting. The police were called, it was really awful.'

At last it seemed father and son could share a common failing, but I wasn't going into my misdeeds. 'Why didn't you ring me?'

Her silence implied *What would be the point?* 'Oh, we sorted it out. Adam didn't seem particularly upset. Made a big joke of things. Of course that's just his defence mechanism. I presume he was shattered, really. He's pubing, too. He needs a father, Martin.'

Then why pick a woman as a partner? I bit my tongue. Probably life with me had put her off men for good. Instead, I promised I would call her from Armidale as soon as I had a place. Duty done, I hung up.

Seiko was perched on the guitar case. I'd decided to take the guitar with me. Maybe I'd have time to play again. I scratched her favourite spot above the tail but she wouldn't purr. 'You'll be alright. Peter will take care of you.' I showed her the shelf stockpiled with her favourite cans of food and set down her meal but she sulked near the dish, her profile disdainful. I let her sleep on my bed that last night. She was the only creature in the entire town who seemed to care that next day I would be humming northwards on the Xplorer.

★ ★ ★

I'd made no advance bookings. Itineraries are for the elderly. At dusk I stepped onto Armidale platform, which with its potted trees and painted seats seemed smarter than I remembered. I asked the cab driver to recommend a city pub.

He was surprised. 'There's plenty of good motels. You'd do better at the Estelle Kramer or Cameron Lodge.'

'Why's that?' I had a fancy for a night or two in one of the old hotels where I used to drink.

'They've modernised the pubs. Ripped out the bedrooms and put in discos and nightclubs. Plenty of noise.'

'Isn't there one left?' How much had this town changed?

'Tatts. University runs it now. Student accommodation, pretty rundown.'

'Tattersalls will suit fine.' I remembered it well, with its Art-Deco façade and old-time atmosphere.

The driver gave a shrug. 'Right you are then.'

We headed in to town while streetlights began to glimmer. I looked out at period houses and return verandas with cast iron lace. In the failing light, old-world gardens, parks and several church spires imitated a 19th century movie set.

'I was here in the '80s. Has the place changed much?'

'In some ways. That recent storm did a fair bit of damage.' He paused at traffic lights and indicated smart house frontages. 'Hail like golf balls. Thousands of insurance claims. Smartened up the place no end.'

'We had a similar effect in Newcastle, after the earthquake.'

'Newcastle? You won't be expecting big city life.'

'I'm not expecting anything.'

'Good way to go. Won't be disappointed.'

He let me out at the Mall and I wandered along to Tattersalls. The ornate entrance with its faded carpet released a familiar smell. Palate-tickling aromas and a friendly racket echoed from the bistro. This would do me for a night or two.

I checked in and dropped off my bags. Downstairs, I ordered a grill, sitting alone like the Invisible Man. Students at other tables argued, laughed and opined. I wondered whether I would ever again feel that sense of magical self-confidence. I lingered a while, reading the wall notes on the old pub's history. As I took the stairs to bed I wondered about the successions of footfalls wearing the carpet thin, and the many hands dulling the banister varnish. Somehow the thought made me feel less alone.

In the morning I looked down on the orange-bricked shopping mall with its locked shops, slatted seats and young tree plantings. Opposite my window I could make out signs for Dymocks and Armidale Art Supplies. They whetted my appetite and I stood lazily imagining my brand-new life, devoid of timetables. There was a help-yourself cereal and toast spread in the upstairs dining room, which had a faded '50s look to its vinyl chairs and formica tables. I had no complaints. A night's accommodation with continental breakfast was only $27.50. My bedroom with its worn red-leaf patterned carpet and wooden bed had kept me warm and dry and I was in the mood to explore. After breakfast I selected one of my jauntier caps and went down into the Mall. I soon saw the changes were superficial. Arched entrances still gave an imposing air to the Post Office, planted foursquare on its corner block. The pillared Courthouse loomed; no suggestion of pre-Millenium reprieve in its stony façade. New book and music shops had opened. I browsed for an hour, then diverted to sit at a country-style table by the vine-covered window of Café Midalé. A waitress brought short black coffee and Greek shortbread. Already a few buskers were performing in the Mall. Through the window I could make out a ruddy-faced Irish caricature of a fellow who tapped his toes as he fiddled. I sat enjoying the sense of novelty. Not a soul in this city knew me.

Outside, I tossed a coin in the busker's violin case. An electric tram was about to set off on the tourist circuit. I hopped aboard for a few hours, then wandered in to a movie

11

theatre. So much for leisure. Already, as 5 o'clock struck, I was worrying about Seiko. I had an unpleasant vision of my tenant in default and the little cat waiting by a locked door. I had to telephone. Peter reassured me, but after dinner, already tired of Tatts' impermanence, I scanned the newspaper. There wasn't much accommodation available. I marked a studio flat at $70 and rang the number.

A woman answered my call. We made a time to inspect the flat and each other. I liked her voice. We'd see. I had an evening to fill. I didn't fancy sitting in the foyer watching communal TV. In my bedroom I took out my guitar and tried a few blues riffs. Music had been my passion once. All I'd wanted was to hold an audience and sing my songs. Applause was sweet. Soft-eyed girls smiled at me. I was headed for stardom. A quiet, subtle shining, that's what I really craved. I paid to have a disc recorded. I told my friends and acquaintances, rang some radio stations, gave away free copies from the stack I'd be paying off for the next two years. I wondered what would happen. In summary, nothing at all. Friends politely accepted their free copy. Shops said they dealt with established suppliers. The community radio stations were pleased to receive a sample and I suppose a

12

few tracks went to air. It's a strange feeling when your dream becomes thin air.

That night I took a while to drift into sleep. Adam was on my mind. Why was he so difficult? Had I failed him? Was it the divorce? I suppose most parents feel accountable for their children's problems. I was far too immature to marry Carol. We were a pair of impulsive children, into bed one day and at the altar the next. Adam was born prematurely, they said. Now I stared into the past and saw how strongly a doubt had lived and spread its tentacles. About me, about Carol, particularly about Adam. Somehow, from the first time I looked at his bruised, misshapen head and heard his fractious wails, my thought had been *Are you my son?* It was a doubt you reject before you dare consider it.

★ ★ ★

I would have to face this issue. I would contact Carol and demand a DNA test. I should have spoken out long ago. My silence said so much about the lack of trust I brought to our relationship.

There must be something to be said for decisiveness for I had a good night's sleep. After breakfast I set out to keep my appointment with Sara Carmody. A bus took

13

me to the outskirts of town. Land stretched away behind a white house with the look of a well-kept farm cottage. A tethered dog barked. Two grazing horses ambled towards the fence line as I followed the unsealed driveway to the front porch, where Sara had stepped out to meet me.

I saw an attractive woman wearing well-cut jeans, a white shirt and a red neck scarf. She looked about thirty.

'Right on time, Martin!'

'I'm an English teacher. We have to be clock-watchers. Peaceful spot here.'

'I like it. A nice mix of town and country life.'

'The horses yours?'

'They're here for agistment but I take them for the occasional canter. The flat's out the back. Would you like to have a look?'

The black and white border collie set up a renewed din as we walked past flowerbeds and a neat vegetable garden. Sara called a reprimand and the dog lay down, nose on paws. Hens fussed behind chicken wire. The door of the flat was open. The place was clean, with a fresh smell of polish and country air. It was self-contained, with a kitchenette, shower and toilet. Sara stood back while I looked around.

'It's pretty small,' she said.

'I don't need much room. This would suit me very well.'

We chatted for a few minutes. I explained that I was taking long service leave; hadn't as yet made plans as to how I would occupy myself.

'Do you plan to write?'

'What makes you say that?'

'You said you're an English teacher.'

'Well, yes. A teacher, not the one who writes the stuff!'

She laughed. 'You seem the type to sit at a computer, turning out the great Australian novel.'

If I had to be typecast, I supposed a writer was acceptable. I smiled. 'Music's more my thing. I plan to compile some of my songs while I'm on leave. And I'll be looking for a part-time job as well.'

'That might be difficult. Armidale's not the best place to look for work.'

I hadn't asked for advice and became business-like. 'I like the place. What do you say to a six month lease?'

She nodded and suggested we go to her house to fix up the details. The interior was as neat and well kept as the outside. She said she lived alone and worked as an independent financial advisor. I was out as far as her age went. Apparently she had a daughter studying

15

at the Newcastle Conservatorium.

'She'll be coming home any day. She rang last week and told me she's dropping out. I've no idea why. This was her final year.'

I had no wish to enter into confidential exchanges and said something platitudinous about pressures on today's youth.

Sara seemed doubtful. 'Her father will expect a much more convincing reason than mere stress. Melissa has a hard job meeting his expectations. But she adores him. She opted to go with him after the divorce.'

Enough. I stood up briskly, then realised I ought to mention Adam. 'Actually, I have a twelve-year-old son. He visits me during the holidays.'

'Not a problem. Can he ride? I give lessons as a sideline.'

'He might want to give it a go.' I really had no idea. Did Adam even like horses? I wrote out a cheque for the first month's rent and Sara handed me my key. I told her I would bring my stuff over the following morning and headed back to the bus stop with a sense of relief. These living arrangements would suit very nicely.

Next morning, I woke to the drone of a vacuum cleaner in the hall outside my room. I dressed and began to gather up my few belongings. I would breakfast at a café before heading out to Sara's. I heard the housemaid's discreet knock, pushed fingers through my tousled hair and opened the door.

'Would you give me five minutes?' But my stomach was lurching and words dried up as I found myself staring into the blue eyes of my first love. Beside a laden linen trolley, she stood surrounded by buckets, brooms and dusters.

'Annie!'

'Hello, Martin,' she said, smiling softly. 'I always knew you'd come back.'

2

Sara

My orderly life was taking a jolt. I was worried about Melissa. Why had my step-daughter dropped out of university? Health? Some academic problem? Last year she was scoring high distinctions. I went down to Newcastle three months ago for her end of year cello performance. Naturally I thought she was wonderful but the applause was genuine. She had everything going for her: talent, looks, brains. Her father was at the recital. We didn't sit together but met up after in the foyer. *You look tired,* I said. He gave his little shrug. *The funding cuts don't make academic life easy. Same workload, fewer staff. But we cope.*

Cope sounded like the right word. He'd aged a lot since I last saw him. He was in his fifties and already developing his father's receding hairline and faint stoop. Seven years on from the divorce, I'd lost most of my resentment towards him. We'd been no different from most couples pushed to the limit with debt, children and lack of time. I worked long hours. Paul had been made head of his department at the university. His crazy first wife was causing trouble. No wonder we fell apart. We were both exhausted. In retrospect, we were two bewildered children raging at the misery we'd got ourselves into. Could we have opted out? I doubt it. At the time, my career was too important and as for Paul selling up and running away to Queensland . . . Anyway, that was all water under the bridge. As we moved towards the coffee urn he rested a tentative hand on my arm. *One and a half sugars?* I felt touched that he remembered such a small detail. I no longer loved him but wasn't ready to share my life again. My dog and horses were enough.

If I'd wondered if letting the flat would intrude on my privacy, I needn't have worried. Martin wasn't a sociable tenant. We'd exchange a few words when I was feeding the chickens or checking on the horses. Sometimes I heard his guitar. I asked if he wanted a phone connected but he said he didn't need one. No car. When I mentioned I was divorced and lived alone, he shied away like a startled rabbit. I was amused. I certainly wasn't looking for anything personal, though I didn't mind having a man on the property. I told him I was driving to Newcastle to collect Melissa, whose cello and luggage would be awkward on the train. He was obliging; he said he would feed Molly and the hens while I was away.

★ ★ ★

When I took canned food over to the flat, Martin invited me in. He was elated, talking loudly, and I noticed the whisky bottle on the table.

'Join me in a drink?'

'I don't like spirits, thanks.'

'Tea? Coffee?'

He was one of those people whose alter ego takes over when they drink. The soul of charm, he served up cheese and olives and brought out his guitar. I watched his long fingers move with delicacy over the strings as he sang blues and ballads with an Irish note of melancholy. There was an emotional quality to the tunes and lyrics, and I was surprised when he said he'd written them himself.

'Are you a professional?'

He said no, but was obviously pleased I thought so. He sang a couple of other songs that spoke to me in a rather intimate way, then launched into a string of very funny anecdotes. I watched the bottle empty, and wondered how long the evening would go on. I admit I was enjoying myself, and it was with an effort that I reminded myself I had to be up early.

Next morning, I was feeding the hens and cantering the horses when Molly's shrill barks brought Martin to the fence. He must have had a frightful hangover. The high-spirited entertainer who'd sung and played and made me laugh was nowhere to be seen. He looked barely awake, and didn't smile when I waved and called to him, 'How's the head?'

His silence made me feel I'd overstepped some mark.

'I came to ask you whether I should walk the dog,' was all he said.

I wasn't keen on asking favours of this morning stranger. Only Molly's reaction to the magic word *walk* made me relent. 'Thanks. She does love to get off the chain. Did you find my note?' He'd seemed so tipsy that I'd scribbled the animals' feeding schedule on a scrap of paper for him.

'Note?' He sounded wary, as though dreading some *billet-doux* from an admirer. What an ego!

'The feeding schedule. I pushed it under your door.'

'I thought we went over all that?'

'Just a reminder.'

'Right. I'll head inside. Have a good trip.'

A self-contained figure, he walked back to the gloom of the studio. In summer it was an inviting oasis of shade but autumn had isolated it in shadow and dead leaves. What had all that sparkle been about last night? It was as though he'd beckoned me to step forward, then slammed a door in my face. I pushed the puzzle aside and became busy with the practical details of departure. There was no reason to say goodbye. His door was shut. For all I knew, he'd gone back to bed. I loaded the boot and backed out of the garage, miserable to be leaving Molly, who was giving a right royal performance on the chain. Thank goodness I'd only be away two days. I really wasn't sure about the carer I'd left her with.

★   ★   ★

I was in Newcastle by mid-afternoon. Melissa had checked us both in at the Motor Lodge overnight. She'd left me a bunch of chrysanthemums in the unit. She's like that; attentive to others in the way of a girl who knows what hurt feels like. Her mother's a disaster! Over and over I had to watch

22

Melissa's hopes collapse as Christmases and birthdays were forgotten. We tried to compensate. Melissa tried to pretend she didn't care.

The flowers were a typical gesture. As I read her card, she came in and gave me a hug.

'I wasn't expecting you till later,' she said. 'I'm awfully sorry I wasn't here when you arrived.'

I hadn't seen her since Christmas. She'd had her hair cut very short and dyed it black. She'd always been on the plump side as a teenager. Now, with her pale skin and dark eyes, she had the look of a waif.

'Have you been eating properly?'

'Of course!'

'Where's your luggage?' I'd planned to leave first thing in the morning.

'At Dad's. Is it a problem?'

'I hoped we could get away early.'

'We can collect the stuff now. Daddy will be home.'

I nodded. 'After dinner. I've been up since five, I'm starving.'

In the restaurant I watched her push food about on her plate while I downed my steak. Back in our room, I changed and did my hair.

'Do I look a mess?' If I had to see Paul, I might as well show him what a treasure he had cast aside.

Melissa just laughed. 'As if!'

Still, I touched up my make-up and added a spray of Chanel for good luck.

★   ★   ★

Paul was living in one of those renovated city buildings. It looked narrow and cramped and no doubt qualified for a harbour view and exorbitant mortgage. He always had expensive taste. The old Jaguar was apparently still going strong. As I parked behind it, I thought of all the trips we'd made together in that car. Suddenly I was reluctant to see him. His new life here could only rub in the sense of failure that divorce leaves.

'Run in and get your bags. I'll wait here.'

'Aren't you even going to say hello to Dad?' She sounded upset.

'What makes you think he wants to say hello to me?'

'You're my *parents*, that's why. Oh, come on!'

'I can't just waltz into his home. Tell him I'm here with you. If he wants to see me, he can come out.' I really didn't want to walk on his polished floors, see his paintings and furniture or set eyes on his new lady.

Melissa ran up the tiled steps and rang the bell. I'd never seen her look so thin. I had no intention of pressing her to finish her degree or forcing explanations she wasn't ready to give, but I needed to know what was going on. The front door opened. After a moment, I saw Paul walk down the steps towards me. I didn't know what to say to him. In another life, we'd still be partners, shopping for groceries together and sleeping side by side. I lowered the window and he bent down at eye level.

'Hello, Sara.'

'Hi, Paul.'

Perhaps I imagined the uncomfortable pause. Fortunately we had Melissa to fall back on. A rectangle of light filled the open front door space as Melissa lugged her cello case down the steps. Paul's methodical movements as he loaded the clumsy instrument reminded me of past trips we'd enjoyed together before the pressures built. I felt strange, thinking how we used to talk so easily. There were no words left now.

'Help me get the bags, Daddy?'

'I'll be there in a minute.'

'Secret parents' powwow?'

As she left us, I signalled Paul to get in to the passenger's seat. 'What's going on?'

'Roz has surfaced. Apart from that . . . ' He was no more able to explain the change in Melissa than I could. I'd never met Roz and had written her off as an erratic mother who regularly broke her daughter's heart. Years of silence and hidden damage; I felt very dubious to hear she was back. But who was I to speak about the needs of an abandoned daughter?

'Of course I'll keep an eye on her.'

'I appreciate that. It's a little awkward here.' Meaning, the new wife wasn't receptive to Paul's daughter. Melissa had told me she wasn't the easiest person to get along with. His intellect had been no help to him in decisions of the heart.

They loaded the luggage and embraced. Melissa fastened the seat belt and waved. As I revved the engine, I called impulsively, 'Look after yourself.'

Paul smiled and gave that comradely little salute of old acquaintance. The difference in our ages had never mattered to me. Now, in the queer glow of evening, his silhouette foreshadowed a tired old man.

★   ★   ★

The trip home wasn't easy. Melissa shared the driving. I felt vulnerable in the passenger seat and anticipated the road ahead in a way that probably got on her nerves. We hadn't spent much time together since our family unit fell apart. She was thirteen then. I knew the consequences of her father's second divorce hit her very hard. She already bore one set of wounds; it seemed terrible that, after working so hard to win her trust, I was a party to her second abandonment. Paul moved down to Newcastle. My work was in Armidale. Melissa visited me in holidays but we'd missed out in recent years. Somehow I couldn't think of her as grown up. In retrospect, my flight to collect her was a mother's protective instinct towards a needy child. She'd still said nothing about giving up her studies. I began to work my way towards that topic but my openers fell flat and I drifted into my own thoughts. It was only on the last stretch of the road, after we'd left behind the steep hill climbs past Tamworth, that she spoke.

'What's on your mind? Are you disappointed in me?'

'No! I've rented the studio. I was thinking about the tenant. Melissa, why don't you tell me what's going on with you?'

'It's the music scene. I don't want any part of it.'

The story spilled out. A cello position in the symphony orchestra had become vacant. Melissa's teacher was a visiting professor and guest conductor of the orchestra. He was a

27

man she respected and admired, and when he'd asked her to audition she was flattered. Extra coaching progressed to a dinner invitation. She hadn't known how to cope.

'So I cooked up this idea with Hugo. We went out and hired formal outfits and bought this phony diamond ring at Big W. So when we got to the restaurant I told the Prof. we were engaged. This was our celebration dinner. He couldn't do a thing about it! Hugo and I made absolute pigs of ourselves, we got drunk, then got the giggles. I felt sick. We had to leave.'

'And the professor was left to foot the bill?' I couldn't help laughing. 'Are you and Hugo an item?'

'He's gay. We're friends.'

Her tuition was abruptly curtailed and another girl was picked for the orchestra. Melissa understood what lay behind the professor's special interest. She'd been devastated. Still, I thought withdrawing from her course seemed extreme. She'd ruined her career prospects.

'You think I ought to have stayed?'

'Life's not perfect.'

'It's right or it isn't.'

'Music, maybe. I think people are a bit less cut and dried.'

Melissa pulled in to a roadside stop. 'You

and Daddy didn't compromise. You got divorced.'

'We did compromise. It wasn't enough.'

'You were so happy to begin with! But the last year was horrible. You were right to split up. And I'm right to leave the Con.'

Why would I argue? I've never appreciated advice that was contrary to my opinions. In her own way she'd learn that right and wrong were often floating definitions. I drove the last hour of the trip. Melissa lowered the seat back and fell into a doze, her lips trustingly apart. However we might try to be adults and equals, I was a mother taking my child to our safe place, home.

★ ★ ★

The uneasy feeling I'd had about Martin turned to panic as I pulled in to the driveway. Molly was gone. I ran to her kennel. Her lead, still attached to the chain, was bitten through. My border collie is an escape artist, fence jumper, chaser of moving bodies. Balls, sheep, cars, road trains, they're all the same to Molly. We've both survived run-ins with angry farmers and stricken drivers until even her best Houdini tactics met their match in the chain. Surely Martin would have seen how securely I kept her tethered. Yet there

29

was the webbing leash, still attached by its clumsy knot, chewed in half. Hadn't he bothered to check? He wasn't in his flat. Perhaps he was out now, searching. I was too angry to care. What a homecoming! I left Melissa to make her own way inside while I began phoning the Pound and local vets. So far my dog hadn't been picked up. She could have gone north or south along the highway. I imagined her headed over green paddocks, eyes bright, pink tongue lolling, herding her charges up hill, down dale. She could be dead in a ditch. I hung up the phone and began to cry. Melissa hugged me. 'Don't worry. We'll find her.'

'I could kill Martin. He's obviously a complete fool. Well, he can move out.'

'There's a man coming up the drive now. He's got Molly.'

Thank God. Through the window I saw the truant, trotting beside Martin on a rope. I raced outside.

'Where the hell was she?'

'I'm not used to dogs. She slipped away about an hour ago. As soon as I noticed I went after her. Found her down the road, rounding up some cows. I had a job to catch her.'

'You've *really* upset Sara.' Melissa scowled.

'I can see that. I'm terribly sorry. I'd got

the dog all ready for a walk, then I remembered I'd left the flat unlocked. She'd gone in a flash.'

I was on my knees, crying, my arms around Molly.

As Martin slipped away, Melissa patted my shoulder. 'Come on. No harm done. I'll make a cup of tea.' As usual she assumed the role of comforter and kind friend.

3

Martin

I kept my distance from Sara and her daughter after the episode with the dog. It was my secret sympathy for tethered animals that let me down. I'd overestimated Molly's complicity in our shared excursions. After a couple of outings she had my measure. One moment of misjudged trust and with gleeful insouciance she was off. No real harm done, except to my relationship with the landlady. Sara obviously needed to cool down.

I played around on the guitar but leisure wasn't all it's cracked up to be. I missed the structure of my working life. As a teacher, I did feel a true caring for my pupils. The playground scuffles, the jeers and fears, the soil and smut that marks a schoolboy's interactions were entrenched in my own heart, as were all the better parts of growing; the intellectual stretching of the mind and the stirring of aspiration. I too once stood in the ranks of choirboys, my scrubbed face pure as a Botticelli angel's. Now I'd failed my charges and cut off my right to work. I missed my students. Even the casual sociability of adult colleagues had filled a solitude that was starting now to drag. I slept late, scanned the pages of the parochial newspaper and cooked up batches of curries and goulash. My determination to go on the wagon had weakened. The whisky intake was a problem but I couldn't summon the strength of will to do anything about it. Instead I sat about replaying my miserable litany of failure. I'd compromised my reputation as a teacher and my book of songs disappointed me. I remembered more ambitious goals than these juvenile lyrics and harmonies implied. It was hard to believe I'd ever had the nerve to put out an album. My personal life was a wreck. If I were to clear up my doubts about Adam, I'd risk alienating him even further and I could just imagine Carol's reaction when I contacted her. The last thing I needed was complications with women. Yet I was surrounded by trouble; Carol furious, Sara upset, and Annie an enigma. That chance meeting had floored me and I'd let myself agree to see her again. Annie, the girl I made love with out at the Metz Gorge. We'd discovered Chaucer, T.S. Eliot and the thrill of passion all at once. What on earth could we have in common now?

In my restless desire to get away from all this, I recognised the symptoms of a full-on binge and pulled back just in time. The night seemed endless. Mournful night creatures hooted and croaked while I lay sleepless, wishing memories and time away. Around dawn I dozed off and a few hours later woke, resolved. I would deal with the lot of it today. I'd shower, shave, get dressed and get straight on to Carol. I'd attend to Annie. In return for the use of Sara's bicycle and her phone, I'd invite my landlady and her pretty daughter to a home-cooked meal. Putting the stamp on decision I rinsed the whisky dregs down the sink and tossed the bottle in the bin.

★   ★   ★

Businesslike in a suit and blouse, Sara said she was on her way to a meeting at nine. I begged my favours anyway. Yes, she said, sounding cool. The phone was in the kitchen. The bike was in the shed. Melissa was asleep. She'd gone before I could mention dinner.

There was no diplomatic way to speak to Carol so I came right out with it. She didn't say a word. I thought she'd hung up.

'Are you still there? I just need to know.'

'Is this your latest excuse, Martin?'

'Excuse?'

'For being such a lousy father. Funny you never said anything when he was born.'

'How could I? I didn't know how I felt.'

'You imply I've always lied to you, but you didn't know?'

'Carol. Let's not argue. I'm clearing up a few issues. I want the test done. I'll pay, of course.'

'Please, Martin!' She sounded genuinely upset. 'Don't do this to Adam. How do you think he'll feel?'

'I don't know. Look, I'll make enquiries and send you the details. There's no point in saying any more.'

'You're dead right. Goodbye.' She slammed down the handset.

Not pleasant but it was done. On to mission number two. I dialled the number Annie had jotted down with her address, and asked to speak to her. There was a pause filled with the racket of family life and the boy returned. His mother was in the shower. Would I leave my number and she'd call me?

I didn't want Annie doing that. 'I don't have the phone on. Just tell her I plan to stop by later today.'

'I'll pass it on.' He sounded as uninterested as any teenager in the agenda of parents. I must have woken Melissa. Wearing a pretty kimono thing, she wandered in, yawning.

'Mum gone?'

'She had a meeting. I'm just making a few phone calls.'

'She's a workaholic. Want a cup of coffee?'

'No thanks. I have to check out a bicycle.'

'Don't you have a car?'

'I can't drive at present.'

'Why?'

'Lost my licence. Drinking.'

'Tut tut!' She laughed. Apparently I qualified for acceptance in the ranks of reckless youth. I left her and went off to inspect the bike and soon saw I wouldn't be going anywhere today. It was an old BSA with Sturmey Archer gears. I'd owned one, as a kid. This was a wreck; tyres flat, chain seized and the brake cable badly frayed. My visit to Annie was off. I went back to the house to report on the state of the bike and phone up about spare parts. The smells wafting from the kitchen were as inviting as a log fire on a winter's night.

'Too late to change my mind about the coffee?'

Melissa was dressed, her hair arranged in spikes and a dark lipstick exaggerating the pallor of her skin. 'Sure. Toast as well?'

I nodded and left her to fiddle in the kitchen while I glanced through Sara's bookshelf. Economic and accountancy texts, several political biographies, Stephen King. On the coffee table, piles of company reports and share market documents suggested she took her work home at night.

'What did you want the old bike for?' Melissa handed me a plate of buttered toast.

'I was going to visit the scene of my first romance.' I felt that jaunty urge to intrigue a girl half my age. 'I'll have to cancel.'

'Let's hire a car. I'm desperate for wheels. There's someone I've got to see.'

'No licence, remember?'

'I'll drive, if you can chip in for the hire fee.'

I was starting to feel manoeuvred. 'Thanks, Melissa, but would your mother want you ferrying me around?'

'I'm not a kid! I'm going to hire a car anyway. Sara's my stepmother, by the way.'

I decided to get the Annie thing over and done with. 'Right. Let's do it.'

'Cool! I'll wash up first. Sara's a fanatic for tidiness. See you in half an hour.'

That was that.

★　★　★

We signed up for the hire car in Melissa's name and she drove me out to Annie's. It was one of those breezy April days when the trees in Armidale are resplendent with colour. Against their blue backdrop, poplars were golden and maples blushed every shade of red. Happy to be out and about, I began to sing a folk song, my yodelling pig ditty, and felt rewarded when Melissa laughed. We drove past paddocks of flowering weeds and wind breaks and, ten minutes after the Saumarez turn-off, swung right onto a country road. The houses began a few kilometres along the way. Annie's place, like the others, was an old weatherboard dwelling. The name on the gate hung crooked and a dated car stood wheel-high in dry grass. I was relieved when Melissa showed no interest in coming in. She offered to collect me in about an hour. She took off, tyres skidding, and I walked slowly towards the house. Kiddies' play equipment lay about. In the vegetable plot a ruff of marigolds edged seeding silverbeet and sprawling tomato foliage. I stooped to acknowledge a ginger cat who returned a lazy blink. A moth-eaten collie gave a warning bark as I approached the sagging veranda. As though she'd been waiting, Annie stepped through the open door. A gathered skirt and loose top gave her a bulky shape. Her hair, still long, had taken on a dry and slightly frizzy look. She wore make-up and I smelt perfume as she came towards me.

'No, Rusty. Down! Where's your car, Martin? I was so pleased to get your message!'

I thought she was about to kiss me and I stepped back.

'A young friend drove me. She's gone off for an hour. So, this is home?'

I couldn't account for the effect this woman had on me. I was suffering all the traditional symptoms of nerves. I really had no idea why I was here.

Giving the snappy dog a wide berth, I followed her inside. The house was archetypal country-style. Bedrooms opened off a central passageway. At the back of the house there was an all-purpose living and eating area extending full width. Annie seemed to live a life of clutter and children. Snapshots, kids' paintings and school notices studded a cork bulletin board, and magnets secured a pile of bills and messages to the fridge.

'Are these two yours?' I was looking at a coloured studio portrait of a boy and girl.

'Bruce and Joanne.' She sounded proud of them.

'And your husband?'

'Ben.' She didn't elaborate. 'So tell me about yourself. Married? Children?'

I nodded. This was hardly the moment to say I was having my son's authenticity checked out. 'Just one. Adam. He's nearly thirteen. He lives with his mother in Sydney.'

'So you're divorced?'

'Not great marriage material, unfortunately. Immature, self-centred. Ask my ex-wife!'

She was suddenly young again as her gaze held mine. She laughed. 'Wives aren't ideal referees. Tell me all about your music.'

'No. I'd rather hear about your family.' I was determined to steer clear of the past.

'Bruce is fourteen. He started last year at TAS. Joanne's at St. Mary's pre-school.'

I was surprised at her mention of The Armidale School. The rundown house and Annie pushing a cleaning trolley around Tatts didn't compute with expensive private education. I wondered why she wasn't using her qualifications. 'Taking a break from teaching, are you?'

'Mmm.' She was vague. 'And you? Holidays?'

'Leave due. I'm back home for a look around.'

'Staying long?'

'No plans. That coffee smells good.'

'I haven't forgotten. Black, sweet, strong.'

How could she remember such a trivial thing? She went to the kitchen area while I stared out at gnarled fruit trees and foraging hens and goats. She used to talk about living on a farm. Perhaps this was her compromise.

On the bookshelf I recognised the old literature course texts. Their faded dust jackets called up vividly a springtime when Annie and I sat under the campus trees, studying together. As Annie set down the cups, she saw me leafing through *The Canterbury Tales.*

'Remember doing that together?'

I smiled at the memory. 'You related best to the tender-hearted prioress. Can you set a mouse trap yet?'

Annie laughed. 'Not really.'

She couldn't bear to kill anything. She saved spiders, geckoes, moths; I'd even watched her put cockroaches out into the garden.

'And you were The Young Squire.' Softly she began to quote.

He was as fressh as is the month of May
Shorte was his gowne, with sleeves longe and wide.
Wel coude he sitte on hors, and faire ride;
He coude songes make, and wel endite,
Juste and eek daunce, and wel portraye and write.
So hote he loved that by nightertale
He slepte namore than dooth a nightingale.

41

'My God! Do you know the whole of *The General Prologue* off by heart?'

'Of course not. Just that bit.'

Her nostalgic tone was a reminder of an overdue debt. I busied myself fitting the books back on the shelf. 'So, how are your parents?'

'Dad had a stroke years ago. He's wheelchair-bound. The old tyrant hasn't really changed but Mum's in her element. She plays the stock market and surfs the Net.'

I was pleased to hear it. Unlike Annie's father, Nina had always made me welcome. Annie went on. 'They're living near Inverell so I don't see much of them. But they'll be at our big family reunion soon. Do come! Mum would love to catch up.'

I had no intention of further get-togethers and was relieved when the telephone interrupted us. We'd met, we'd talked. As Annie took the call, I checked my watch. Fifteen minutes until Melissa collected me. Tentacles of domesticity stretched from the shabby cushions and faded curtains. I had an urge to close my eyes and rest.

'If you keep her off the road I'll come straight away,' Annie concluded as she hung up. She turned swiftly, nostalgia forgotten.

'It's our poor old horse. The paddock fence

42

is full of holes. I'll have to go and get her.' She ran outside and came back with a bit and bridle. As she dealt with windows and keys, I was just another detail. 'I'm so sorry to rush off.'

In fact, I preferred this quick end to things. 'Don't worry, Annie. I'll wait on the veranda.'

She insisted I read the paper, have another coffee. 'If I'm not back when you go, just slam the front door. And don't forget the family reunion. I need to talk to you.'

She mentioned a date and time, and she was gone.

Alone, I did a little spying. In a typically littered boy's bedroom, the bookshelf was packed with *Encyclopaedia Britannica*, *National Geographic*, and a row of other references. The furniture was rough and the floor boards bare, but a plethora of sporting trophies and certificates suggested an accomplished lad. He must be an adolescent; a tube of Clearasil ointment lay on the dressing table. Feeling I'd overstepped the bounds of privacy, I avoided the other bedrooms and went back to the main living area to contemplate the many prints of children playing with pets, celebrating birthdays and smiling from formal school photographs. I realised I hadn't a single picture of Adam. Carol had the records from his early years, while I'd never thought to film our miserable holidays together.

It was a relief to hear Melissa's toot. Avoiding the dog, I pulled the door to and followed the path to the gate. *Windsong* swung there on its loose hand-painted board. A poetic enough name for a country cottage complete with children, a garden, pets contented with lives of placid restraint — but where in this pretty picture was the tempestuous Annie I remembered?

Melissa dropped me back at Sara's. I waved as she drove away, then walked on to my unit. A horse ambled to the fence and I paused, meeting its long-fringed gaze in cautious appraisal. Molly, dozing on the chain, lifted her nose as I approached and gave a bored bark.

'What are you up to, Molly? Dreaming or plotting?' Her long tail brushed the grass. She would have liked a walk but I didn't dare try that again. Inside, I sank onto the sofa, feeling flat and disappointed. Annie's life mystified me. The past blurs and people disappear in complicated networks, as though they abandon a personal existence. Annie was an old photograph, contemplated by a traveller who sits alone on a winter's night. I felt profoundly lonely. I *have measured out my life with coffee spoons.* In my case, whisky shots. It wasn't much to be proud of. Needing company, I reached for my old guitar. How easily our bodies fitted! My fingers strayed without effort through a blues improvisation. *He coude songes make!* If only human interaction was as easy.

4

Sara

Melissa was supposed to join me for Martin's dinner invitation, but she didn't show up. She'd told me about his cancelled licence so I thought it better to take sparkling apple juice which he accepted with a quizzical look. At least it helped quench the effects of red-hot curry. I declined a second helping.

'Pity Melissa couldn't make it.'

'She has her own life to lead.' I didn't say that since she'd had the use of the hire car, I'd hardly seen her. 'She left here when she was thirteen. When Paul and I broke up she went to live with him.'

He seemed surprised to learn she was my stepdaughter. 'You must have been very young to marry a divorcee and take on a child?'

'I had no idea what I was getting into. Paul was a lecturer at university and I had a good job in an accountant's firm. We never stopped running.'

'Very like my own situation. Dash to work,

hurry home, pick up the babysitter.'

'Rush to the supermarket, cook tea, fly off to Jazzercise. Paul and I had seven years together. Some of it was good, but the bad won.'

'Carol had post-natal depression. Neither of us had a clue what was going on. I wasn't any support. Coping with my own horrors.'

I heard the regret in his voice. 'What happened?'

'Carol got into those personal development courses and did a degree in psychology. One day she took Adam and left.'

I knew about the sense of hurt and failure that divorce entails but he didn't want to pursue that topic. His next comment took me by surprise.

'How was it, inheriting a stepdaughter?'

I felt quite offended that he'd think I only accepted Melissa as a hanger-on.

'She was a dear little girl. I was so sad when she went to live with Paul.'

'You don't subscribe to the *blood's thicker than water* idea?'

'It's a cliché. Thousands of kids have stepparents. Surely you're not saying a child's only loveable if she's our own flesh and blood?'

Martin ran his fingers through his hair. 'I'm not sure what I'm saying. I find the whole

47

issue confusing. A woman never has to wonder. Adam and I are chalk and cheese. I've just asked for DNA testing.'

I wished he hadn't told me. I'd assumed the dinner was his way of apologising for the episode with Molly. I was willing to start again on cordial terms, but his attitude made me wonder if he had any idea about a child's feelings. Surely his son would feel rejected, whatever the outcome.

'Adam must feel you're his father. Would you want to disown him if your suspicions are right?'

He disliked that. 'Of course not! I just need to know whether he's my son.'

He sounded remote and for some reason I was angry. Perhaps I'm unduly sensitive to this question of surrogate parenting. Somewhere in the background I have always felt the presence of Melissa's shadow-mother. Paul had said the pair had traced each other and were in contact. Was she the reason behind Melissa's secrecy? She hadn't said a single word to me about their reunion.

The silence between us began to feel uncomfortable. Martin wouldn't drop the subject.

'A man's genetic child is his immortality, in a sense.'

I was listening with growing disbelief to all

this obsessive talk of paternity. He didn't strike me as a man who would even want a family.

'You want to live for ever?'

'I don't think a woman quite understands.'

On that irritating note, we dropped the subject of children. Martin made coffee, opened a box of after-dinner mints, tuned his guitar and sang a few of his songs.

As I listened to his melodious voice, I decided he seemed sensitive; a man of tenderness and good will. Yet I'd seen the empty bottles, he'd almost lost my dog and he apparently cared little for the unfortunate boy he was about to drag through some murky past. When he laid the guitar aside, I stood up. 'Thanks for the meal. Want help with the dishes?'

He declined and we said good night. Melissa wasn't home. I waited until midnight, then went to bed. She came home not long after, but though my light was on, didn't stop by to say goodnight.

I was beginning to wish I hadn't let the flat. Perhaps I was more of a hermit than I realised. I felt impinged on and missed the solitude of my single life. Animals share their warmth and comfort without a price. But humans . . . Martin seemed an odd bod and Melissa's secretive manner was hurtful. She asked for nothing, shared nothing and offered me only trivialities. She made no plans to work or study, ate like a sparrow and spent more time hanging around my tenant than I felt was appropriate. They were both people with time on their hands. Perhaps I was envious. My own work hours varied but they imposed a schedule on my life. As well, I had to tend the animals and garden, see to the usual housework, laundry, shopping and finances. There wasn't much space left. I wasn't sleeping well. A kind of anxiety, a whirling of the thoughts, started as soon as I turned off the light. Milk drinks and soothing music didn't help. I was having unpleasant dreams. The details never remained; only the lingering sense of apprehension.

I tried exercise. On a day when Melissa was out as usual and Martin was working on the bike, I took Molly for a long walk along the Waterfall Way. It was a beautiful afternoon; horses frolicking in the green paddocks, the golden poplars shining, birds arrowing northwards. Yet this beauty couldn't lift me. Leaves would fall, horses and sheep would stand despondent in the fog. My steps lagged and Molly's tail drooped as she sensed the walk was curtailed.

How the rest of the day dragged! I tried all the usual remedies to mask a sad mood but the sense of life's futility persisted. By evening, I found myself sunk in self-pity, turning the pages of the old photo album created at a time when we were a family. I stared at Paul and myself in wedding finery, at plump Melissa folk dancing with other children on that trip we made to Old Sydney Town. Here was our run-down house before we did the renovations. There was Melissa in school uniform, her teeth in bands, her hair pulled back in a ponytail. After that page the rest were blank. I slammed the album shut and pushed it back into the cupboard beside the old shoebox of unmounted snapshots. I ran a hot bath, took valerian and opted for an early night.

My peace of mind wasn't gained so easily. Dreams came vividly, endlessly. Pursued in some sort of war zone, I had to evade landmines, traps, barbed wire, as on and on I ran with my entrusted cargo in my arms. Up mountains, over bridges, through black tunnels and fog-shrouded paddocks where passive animals huddled, the unending pursuit continued until, beaten and exhausted, I had to concede, aban-don my shrouded bundle beneath leafless trees and walk away.

I sat up in bed, sobbing. I felt a tight pain in my chest and instinctively pressed my hands to my heart as I walked over to the cupboard, reached up to the high shelf and lifted down the crammed shoebox. Sitting on the side of the bed, I began searching through the random photos for the one that had always been too private and too painful to display. There it was; a black and white snapshot of a girl, about sixteen. She stood in a floral dressing gown, a new-born baby pressed against her shoulder so that only the dark crown of hair showed above the baby blanket. I sat staring at myself and my tiny daughter, Shannon; the little girl I'd briefly been allowed to hold before I was counselled to be wise, to be practical, to be unselfish and give her to proper parents who could offer her advantages I couldn't possibly supply. My expression, sombre and withdrawn, already reflected a waiting sorrow. Like every mother who loses a child, I would learn to numb the pain. Each passing birthday put another year's distance between us. My daughter was somewhere, growing into a stranger I would never know. Yet that old photograph bound us as closely as when I'd felt her arms and legs swim gently in my womb. Her defenceless head nestled against me and my arms clasped her to my swelling breasts, already bound up to suppress my milk.

She was kept away from me after that. They said it would be easier. I heard other babies cry and craved to hold Shannon. I didn't give a thought to her father, even when the husbands came with smiles and flowers and kisses. I'd cared more about the grass stain on my skirt than I had for that impulsive clumsy boy. Why connect him with my baby? It was I who gave birth to her. While visitors sat by other beds, I lay turning the pages of magazines displaying glamorous models and exotic clothes few people could afford. I liked the distance this unreal world created. Perhaps I would find a place there. For I knew the kind world of my trusting childhood was gone. Bright days, safe nights, Christmas surprises, all over. Two truths were left. I was alone. I should never trust too deeply. Her loss would always be my warning.

Overcome by memories, I sank weeping onto the bed, thinking in amazement, Why mourn all over again, like this? Why long to know Shannon, this young woman with a new name, living her own life of unknown joys and sorrows in some strange city? All this was supposed to be lost in deep memory banks one never visits. Somehow Martin's delving had set off my own buried questions. Rocking and sobbing, I kept asking myself, Who is she? Who is my daughter?

I heard Melissa and felt her consoling arm around me. Without a word I offered her the photo.

'It's you?' That was all she said and I nodded dumbly. She seemed to understand. Perhaps her own abandonment as a small girl had sharpened her instinctive knowledge of loss. We sat and I allowed her tender fingers to stroke my hair as though she was a mother easing away my nightmare. When I was calm, she made tea and set two cups down on the bedside table, beside the photo I'd propped there. I saw my clock had stopped at midnight. 'What time is it?'

'One thirty.'

'You were late home?'

'Mmm. Tell you tomorrow.' She settled me down, tidied my covers, and turned off the light. 'Happy dreams,' she said. That was how I'd always tucked her up until she left home to go with Paul. I nodded, closed my eyes and, exhausted, slept soundly after that.

★　★　★

We talked closely next morning. Others may admire our successes but our weakest moments establish friendship. Knowing the hurt she'd suffered herself as a child, I wanted Melissa to understand why I gave Shannon to strangers.

'Teenage girls of my generation had none of today's support. We believed we were

54

guilty. How could we argue? We only had feelings to pit against their logic. I'm not even sure their advice was so bad. Most of those adopted babies were wanted desperately. Who's to say?'

'It seems cruel, making a mother give up her child.'

'Yes. It was. They thought it was best for the baby.'

Melissa considered that, then said thoughtfully, 'I wonder if my mother felt like that when she left?'

I had no desire to disillusion her. 'Aren't you in touch with her now? You could ask her.' What would I say if my own daughter confronted me with such a question?

Melissa stared at me. 'How do you know I'm seeing Mum?'

So that was why she'd taken to using my Christian name! All my hard work in the maternal role apparently couldn't compete with the birth bond. I had to remind myself that Roz, that selfish, adolescent woman, was only a construct in my mind. Melissa's hurt and Paul's resentment had helped build it, but now it faltered. We ought not to be rivals for Melissa's allegiance. Perhaps there were factors Paul had never understood.

'Paul mentioned you'd received a few letters. Where is she living now?'

'Here. I visit her most days.' She looked at me, guilty as an unfaithful wife and I felt ashamed. What child's love should dwell in compartments? Her mother and I weren't in a contest for Melissa's heart.

'Really? How is she doing?'

Delighted now, as though she could confess her secrets, she ran to her room and brought back her wallet. She drew out a snapshot of her mother and I saw an older Melissa, watchful, tough, clinging hard to youth. The curly mane of hair, the tight, off the shoulder top, the blazing smile all suggested the sexuality I'd always found threatening. Now I remembered. Paul's tales about his first wife shared a message I had better heed. A sexual woman spelt trouble and pain all round. Restocking my wardrobe, I remembered how I used to cast my eyes over black lace and maroon satin, sigh and deliberately buy cotton undies and dainty floral nighties. The breath of that sleeping child penetrated our bedroom walls whenever we made love; a silent, pleasant enough love, hardly memorable. When that began to happen less, I read the magazine articles on executive stress. They reminded me Paul was an older man with a demanding job. After all, I was busy too.

It's easy to drape your own attitude around

the shoulders of an absent figure. Roz was the villain in the background. But had I ever known desire with Paul? Put it this way; would I have chosen Paul if I'd wanted wild sex? He was an intellectual man, more comfortable with analysis than abandon. I had supposed his marrying a woman like Roz was a classic case of *opposites attract;* a cliché that failed to include the clashes and disasters likely to be sparked by different natures. If the romantic spark between us hardly glowed, our relationship was safe and I needed safety. I see that now. I'd made one dreadful mistake but I was a quick learner. Nothing like that would ever disrupt my peace again. Whatever the past implied, I would in future guard my finances, my animals, and my emotions. Particularly those! I had a real instinct for those people who wanted more than what I had to offer. Clients who slipped in a casual dinner invitation met with exactly the same response from me as doorknockers toting religion, raffle tickets or roof inspections.

But when you love someone, it's harder to say No. Melissa was waiting for me to respond. Ignoring my impulse to snatch the picture and tear it up, I asked where Roz was living. I didn't like the answer.

'She rents a caravan up the road, at Pembroke.'

'And is she with anyone?'

'Her partner died last year. She says he had some horrible blood disease. He just bled to death one night. She was there, it was terrible, there was nothing she could do to stop it.'

No home, no money, no job, a lover, tragedy, groans and cries, Roz, knee-deep in pools of crimson blood. Yes, I could imagine her in that scenario. And now, alone again.

Melissa's eyes shone with pleading. 'It sounds awful,' I made myself say.

'Mum's had such bad luck! I think she's changed, Sara. I know things about the past. Dad's told me. But that was ages ago. She came down to Newcastle by train and arranged to meet me. She gave me this.'

She held up her wrist. I'd noticed the charm bracelet with its dangling animals; something off a street stall. She never took it off. I had to nod approvingly even as I thought a bit of junk jewellery was a poor exchange for a whole childhood of neglect.

'Is she why you wanted to come back to Armidale?'

Calm as I sounded, my world was rocking. *I'm your mother!* How dare this woman think that with one visit and a trinket she could make up for all the care

58

and love I'd given Melissa.

'Of course not! I told you what happened.'

'It seems a coincidence.' I don't like surprises. This reappearance of Roz felt particularly unpleasant. I neither knew nor trusted her, yet she clearly retained a power over her daughter that worried me. For this situation I had no hedging strategy. If I spoke my mind, Melissa would turn her back on me. She needed to forgive her mother. Unless I co-operated, she would quite likely decide to eliminate me, along with that whole painful past.

'I'm sure you'd like her, Sara. I was wondering, could I ask her round some time? I thought we could all have a barbecue; you know, nothing fancy, Mum's not into that sort of thing.'

She was referring to my penchant for doing things in style. I'm a good cook when I'm entertaining. Though it's a rare event these days, I make sure a dinner party is an event my guests won't forget. Melissa needn't have worried! I had no desire to get out the gold-edged Wedgwood for Roz.

Without meaning to, Melissa turned the knife. 'You'll like Mum! After all, you've both got things in common. I mean, you don't have husbands, and you both had to give up a child. So, when can I ask her over?'

59

I felt quite sick. 'Well. I've got a lot of work on this week. Let's talk about it after that.'

She kissed me then; a loving, spontaneous kiss, as though it was her birthday and I'd found the one and only gift her heart desired.

5

Martin

I'll never forget that first bike ride out to Annie's. How had I overlooked the fact that it was over twenty years since I'd regularly cycled? I'd fixed The BSA. It was a lovely autumn day and I'd thought an hour would cover the trip. But it was late afternoon when I pushed through the half-dozen parked cars and staggered up Annie's path to join her family reunion. There were people everywhere. When a stranger thrust a stubby of cold beer into my hand I forgot all good resolve and drank like a parched desert explorer. At that satisfying moment I cared not one whit about the past.

For a while I sat in the shade of an old lemon tree, watching the melee of children, cats, dogs and ducks. A big tent had been set up in the garden and balloons fluttered from the veranda where I recognised Douglas, Annie's white-haired father. He was seated in a wheelchair, staring past all the activity as though his mind was elsewhere. I couldn't see her mother, or Annie herself. The bellowing, thickset chap in the white polo shirt and straining shorts must be her brother, plus a kilo or two for each of the sixteen years it had been since we last met. Eight or nine kids argued over the batting order as he oversaw a hapless game of cricket. I was glad of this break before the social niceties began. I had the extraordinary thought that, if I'd married Annie, this could be my life. Could I ever have become one of these family people, brimming with jolly togetherness? Would I have learned to bowl a cricket ball to Adam? But there would have been no Adam if I'd chosen Annie.

'Martin!' She was waving from the veranda steps. 'So you made it!'

I gave her a wry rundown on the bike ride and she laughed.

'Come and meet everyone.' She led me to the wheelchair, speaking to her father as though he was a child. 'Dad, do you remember Martin? We used to go out together. He's come to share the day.'

Cold eyes swivelled to meet mine. With a grunt he stared back into the distance.

'He's confused. Come and see Mum.' Annie turned the wheelchair from the slant of the sun's rays as though tending a baby in a pram. 'She's in the kitchen.'

As I followed her along that long passageway, I could see the mountain of visitors' luggage, clothes and sleeping bags that littered the rooms.

At the sink, Annie's mother turned from washing dishes. 'My goodness, the one that got away.' She dried her hands and looked me up and down. 'Still skinny, I see. My chocolate crackles and ginger crunch didn't do you much good.'

'I faded away without you, Nina.'

She giggled, brushing back her white fringe with a flirtatious gesture. We'd always got along well. She'd hardly changed at all — if anything, seemed lighter, as though invigorated by her new powers. They'd had one of those old-fashioned marriages where the husband's word was law. He'd been heavy-handed with his children and my courting of his daughter hadn't won me any points with him. Little as I'd had to do with him, avoiding and even fearing him a little, now I wondered what sort of helpless hell he had to suffer in that chair, and whether an inexorable balance demanded that one's victories were stolen at the cost of another's defeat. *Poor old bugger!* I thought. I'd go back and talk to him later.

'I'm going to find the kids,' Annie said. 'I've told them all about you, Martin.'

Told them what? I didn't think our youthful affair would be appropriate to discuss with her children. Nina sensed my confusion.

'Annie always kept up with your music, you know. She was thrilled to hear you'd done a recording.'

'I had no idea she knew about that.'

'Oh yes. Gave copies to all her friends. I suppose you're famous now? We're provincial, we don't know what's going on in Sydney.'

She didn't realise I'd given away big-city life years ago. I was out of my depth. The thought of a former girlfriend stealthily tracking my life and my actions disturbed me.

'No, I don't perform now; not for many years. The muse moved on.'

'That's a shame.'

'Not good enough at music, or marriage. But at least Annie's happy?'

I wondered. There'd been no mention of the husband. Surely he was here?

Nina's shrewd eyes regarded me like a magpie assessing a titbit. 'Ben's not the intellectual type,' she said obscurely. 'Mind you, an excellent father. Have you met? There he is.' She pointed through the window and I recognised the burly fellow, my saviour with the beer bottle, crouched down with another man. They were peering under a dilapidated

64

old vehicle. 'Talking shop as usual.' She sounded resigned.

'Is he a mechanic?'

'No. He works at the Hillgrove mine. Cars are his hobby.'

I noted her fastidious tone when she referred to the mine. Annie's parents, like my own and so many ageing white Australians, had always maintained snobbish cultural distinctions as rigid as the inherited class or caste systems of traditional societies. I produced a neutral smile and said I would stroll out and introduce myself.

I decided to go the front way and have a word with poor old Douglas. It had been clear he didn't remember me; probably just as well. He didn't deserve to be segregated so I approached the wheelchair with a cheery 'Lovely day!'

I was preparing further banalities when the old man turned his head and fixed me with his gaze. One fist began to strike his knee again and again and there was rage in the slurred syllables as he spat and dribbled the same words repeatedly. *Bastard! Bastard!*

I had no idea why my appearance had invoked such melodrama or what the old man meant, but he'd awakened the dread of a callow boy who'd kept Annie out beyond the curfew hour. He may have confused me with one of his own children to whom he bore a grudge. I hurriedly backed off, terrified he might take another stroke and die right there in his chair.

Ben, in a red-checked flannelette shirt, was still inspecting the lower reaches of the vehicle. When he saw me he stood up, wiped off grime on his jeans and crushed my palm in a warm handshake.

'I'm Martin Ainsworth. Thought I should come and introduce myself.'

'G'day, glad you could come. Ever seen one of these?' He patted the bonnet affectionately. 'Chevvy. Love to know her history. Thinking of doing a conversion to 12 volt — no more hard starting, get rid of the yellow headlights. Can't decide whether to use an alternator or generator. What d'you reckon?'

'Beyond me!' I was about as familiar with those gadgets as I imagined Ben would be with Cockentrice at a Chaucerian feast.

He stood fingering his short black beard. 'Can't make up my mind which way to go. Guess a generator. I'd have to change the bracketing if so. Regulator'd need rewiring but. You one of Annie's cousins?'

'No relation. We were at Uni together. I'm a high school teacher here on leave. Guess I'm gate-crashing.'

He laughed his deep, amiable chuckle. 'No worries! What're you drinking? Plenty of cold ones in the fridge. Hey, Bruce! Come over here and get our visitor a beer. Martin, meet my son. Doing first rate at school he is.'

An acne-ridden lad said something to his friends and sidled over. Thin and lanky, he was outfitted in brand-new clothes with the Billabong name brand. Ben touched his shoulder much as he'd fondled the car. 'Martin's a teacher, you make sure you show him all those certificates. Real smart, even if you don't know a jack from a wheel brace.'

Embarrassed by his father's praise, the boy shuffled feet that looked unnaturally large in the pristine Adidas shoes. I guessed he was a couple of years older than Adam.

'Can I get you a beer?'

'Not right now.' I was keen to get away myself. Cars have never been a major interest of mine. 'How about showing me those awards? For sport, are they?'

He shook his head, glancing over to his friends. 'I don't do sport. They're State awards. Maths and science. And I won a writing competition. Got two hundred dollars.'

'Well done. What about music? I play the guitar.'

'I've got one. Can't play, never had lessons.'

67

'Maybe I could slip you a few while I'm in town?' I was surprised to hear myself make the offer. Perhaps knowing the financial sacrifices his parents must be making on his behalf made me want to help a little bit.

'Thanks, but the guitar's wrecked. Joanne busted it, fooling around. 'Scuse me, my friends are waiting.' He glanced at his father and was gone.

'They want everything new at his age.' Ben was resigned. 'Nothing wrong with that guitar that I couldn't fix with a spot of PVA. Wouldn't suit his mother but.'

'Why's that?' It seemed an odd remark.

He shrugged. 'Annie gives them the best. Bruce goes to The Armidale School. Annie's got her mind set on New England Girls for Joanne. I guess she knows. But I'm doing all the overtime I can and the money doesn't grow on trees.'

'What do you do for a crust, Ben? An engineer?'

'No, I'm over at Hillgrove. The antimony mine.'

'I thought that dried up years ago?'

'That was the gold. The antimony's still going. The place would be a ghost town without it.'

'I'd like to see it some time.'

My interest seemed to please him. 'I'll run

you out there one day. Not a lot to see. There's a display about the old days in the museum. Shows you what a risky game mining was, back then.'

'I imagine there are still risks.'

'A man has to go where the work is.'

I felt sorry for him. He seemed a decent man. How could a miner pay private school fees for his children? Adam's school fees were shared by Carol and myself, and even then it was a hefty commitment.

Ben waved to someone in the distance. 'Come and meet my brother. I'd better start the barbecue. You staying?'

I was at a loss to reply. I'd been dreading the return journey. Neither the bike nor myself were up to another marathon that evening. I explained the situation and Ben laughed. 'Out of condition, mate! Make a night of it here — the kids are going to pile in to the tent and there's a ton of spare sleeping bags. You can stow the bike on the ute and I'll drop you off on my way to work.'

That was the exact moment I decided I liked Ben.

★   ★   ★

The rest of the day passed as these occasions do, with paper plates, sausages and charred steak, and attempts to converse with people who preferred sport, cars and garden projects to music or literature. I'd hardly seen Annie. Nina and I had a good chat and it was as Annie had reported. Her mother seemed much happier in spite of her husband's dependent state. I avoided the old man after that one bizarre encounter and slouched around the edges of the party, downing beers that people kept giving me. I thought the kids would never go to bed. They charged about, waving torches, shouting and screaming, while the older boys gathered around Bruce's computer to play some violent action game. At some ungodly hour, parents began to settle their offspring in the big tent and bed down themselves. I helped myself to a spare sleeping bag and opted for a bunk in Bruce's empty room.

I was half asleep when the door opened and I saw the outline of a woman. Holding a glass, she came towards the bunk and I sat up, alarmed. The last thing on my mind was a tête-à-tête with Annie. She lurched closer and I could smell the wine on her breath when she spoke.

'Tell me what you really thought, when you opened your hotel door and saw me standing there?'

I had to say something but I had no

intention of telling her she'd sparked off a lot of memories and regrets. 'Well. I was surprised.' That was certainly true.

'Fancy! I was surprised too, when you upped and offed without saying goodbye.'

I did not want to have this conversation, now or ever. My heart went into overdrive, checking the exits of my body as if it might escape and go scuttling into the smallest rat hole it could find. Cowardly excuses crowded my lips.

'Listen. Honestly, it was nothing to do with you, Annie. This place, this small-town life, I had to get away.'

'Is that right? And now you're back. Well, fancy that! I loved you!'

Her accusing tone would bring relatives crowding in to investigate. I snapped on the bedside light and jumped out of the bunk, nearly tripping inside the bag as I shuffled over to close the door. What could I offer her? My mind was blank.

She started crying; deep sobs, distorting her face.

'Annie, listen, I loved you too. I often thought about you. I heard you'd married, and then you had a baby. I assumed you'd found happiness. We both moved on.'

'How did you know I married?'

'I can't remember. The word reached me

somehow. It was a long time ago.'

'And I suppose you thought I'd married a common labourer on the rebound?'

'What a rotten thing to say. How drunk are you?'

'About as drunk as you were when you whispered all those lies in my ear.'

Her red face and wild dishevelled hair made her look ugly and no longer young. Yet this was the intense, passionate Annie I knew. Her demands felt intimate, as though the past had slipped into present tense.

I made my tone cold and distancing. 'Why would I look down on your husband? I don't even know him.'

'Ben always wanted me, kept after me. A girl likes that. I had him on a string. He didn't know I was in love with you. He's not a brain, like you. But he was there for me when you left town.'

'Annie. For God's sake, leave the past alone.'

'Of course. That's just the kind of thing you would say.'

I preferred her scorn to tears. Perhaps the scene was over. I profoundly hoped so. But no, she had more to say.

She sounded broken-hearted. 'Oh Martin . . . If only you hadn't come back.'

I couldn't stand any more of this. My

relationships tended to lead to this point of reproachful claim, and I usually knew the way to put a civil end to things. So what if Annie had been my first, perhaps my deepest love? Now I hesitated to use that word, no longer knowing quite what it meant. 'You're right. It was a mistake. I won't come again.'

'Sorry, you can't just walk away now. There's one thing you need to know. My children will never have to go without, the way Ben and I do.'

Now what? Surely she wasn't asking me for money? I knew the look of struggle. It surrounded me in the meagre furniture, faded bedding, fraying floor mats. What was that to do with me? We'd met again through coincidence and the sooner I extricated myself from this family the happier I'd be.

'Haven't you wondered about Bruce?'

'No.' As far as I could see, he was a spotty teenager, possibly picked on at school. But he had parents who seemed to devote their lives to his future. Whether he would thank them for their sacrifices was nothing to do with me.

It was time to make my exit clear. 'I promise I'll be gone first thing. I'll never trouble you again.'

'No,' she said again. 'You owe us something. You're a teacher. You could help Bruce with his studies.'

'That would be quite inappropriate.' I was non-negotiable. This was ridiculous and the thought came to me that she was unhinged.

But as she was about to argue further, the door opened.

'So that's where you were,' Ben said fondly. 'Coming to bed, love? Your parents have turned in.'

'Did they need anything?' The solicitous daughter turned to me. 'Mum and Dad are in our room tonight. We have the settee.'

'And the springs are shot.' Ben waved to me. 'I'll be away about six, Martin.'

'Don't worry, I'll be awake.' There was no risk I'd sleep in!

★   ★   ★

I slept fitfully and was up the moment I heard Ben move around next morning. The living room was a dark barn of huddled bodies. I could make out Annie's shrouded figure, sound asleep. Outside, mist gave the house an insubstantial look. With huge relief I loaded the bike onto Ben's ute.

We didn't talk a lot on the trip to town. I stared out at foggy paddocks where sheep stood wrapped in quaint coats. Bleak nights were upon us. We passed the airport and approached town, where I directed Ben

74

towards Sara's address.

'This'll be handy,' he said, swinging right to drive past the English brick buildings of the Boy's School.

'Handy?'

'For Bruce. He can walk to your place after school.'

I felt I was in some repertory where they'd forgotten to tell me what part to play.

'Sorry?' I said. 'What are you talking about?'

'The music lessons. I told Annie you'd offered. She thinks it's a good idea.'

'Look, I could be moving on soon. I can't make promises.'

'Not to worry. I'll get that guitar fixed and just do what you can. Start this week?'

There wasn't much I could do. I set a day and time.

6

Sara

At first I managed to stall off that wretched barbecue with excuses of a heavy week at work. That was true. My business was expanding. My books confirmed that in six months I'd have surpassed my income goal for the full year. My car would be paid off. I'd be well on the way to clearing the mortgage balance. I could even think about a decent holiday; Rome or Paris, with visits to a few of the designer boutiques. I appreciated beautiful fabric and fine design. My body thrilled to the caress of satin, the drape of fine wool, the earthiness of linen.

I was going out to dinner with a prospective client. The young woman was a lawyer who'd recently joined a partnership in town. I was looking forward to the evening and went to a fair bit of trouble to dress. Melissa was home, watching the news, as I put the finishing touches to my hair and make-up and went out into the living room.

'What do you think?' I did a pirouette. 'Not over the top?'

It was the first chance I'd had to wear my silk taffeta Perri Cutten jacket, camisole and pants. I waited for her comments. As a little girl she'd always loved to watch me dress, and now I'd have happily let her borrow anything of mine.

All she said was, 'That must have cost a lot.'

I felt defensive. 'Only what I'd usually spend on a decent outfit. You can't look like an Op Shop reject in my job.'

She said nothing. I guessed she was thinking *Like poor Mum*. She turned back to the news, where images of haggard Middle Eastern faces peered through the wire fence of a detention centre.

'It's wrong,' Melissa said. 'Caged like animals. People in this country ought to share the wealth around.'

Her unsubtle message put me thoroughly offside. Melissa was spending all her free time with Roz and hardly a day went by without some new report on her mother's difficulties. Quite frankly, I didn't want to know.

'Are you trying to make some point here?'

'I was thinking how tough it is for Mum,' she said.

It was hard to hide my resentment. Did she really expect me to feel compassion for that woman, who'd created her own problems and

77

hurt a lot of people in the process, not to mention stealing Melissa's love and loyalty? My stepdaughter was setting herself up to be hurt all over again. I didn't believe the leopard had changed its spots.

'Melissa, does it occur to you she didn't spend all the years I did studying and passing exams? What about the hard work I've taken on, running my own business?'

'People like you and Dad can deal with pressure.'

I felt angry. Melissa had never gone short of anything material. We'd seen to that. Now apparently she lumped Paul and me together as some sort of élite.

'We're not all victims, Melissa. We make our own lives.'

'Like those people?' She indicated the distorted faces pressed to the wire. It was as close as we'd come to an argument, and tension swelled between us until she stood up and walked out of the room. I went off to meet my client, feeling thoroughly out of sorts. All through the evening, as we ordered a vintage wine, enjoyed a high-class meal and discussed the various investment options she was considering, I felt reproached, as though the underprivileged of the world cast hungry gazes upon our laden table.

Of course people are affected by accidents

of geography. But I also knew that, rich or poor, none of us gets through life unscathed. We control what we can, some more ably than others, but life still throws that curved ball. So I was doing well, and Roz less so. Melissa had no right to reject my life and values. There was nothing inherently superior in her mother's haphazard past. I wasn't going to pity her because she had no assets and had lost husbands and partners along the way. Yet I knew Melissa and I were on the brink of a rift.

I waited a day or so, chose a quiet moment, and proposed we have our barbecue. It was pathetic to see her pleasure.

'Thank you, Sara! I'll tell Mum today. She'll be thrilled.'

I doubted that. Why would Roz want to meet me? I married her husband and raised her child. Now I was well off, independent and ten years younger than she was. No, I couldn't imagine Roz delighting in this invitation. I didn't care. This was for Melissa.

'Let's ask Martin, too,' she suggested.

'You can if you want.'

'Don't you like him?'

How to answer? I thought he was an odd person. All that talk about his son had put me off, and he had an annoying tendency to sound superior. The other day, when I used some commonplace expression, *once in a blue moon*, I think it was, he went into a peculiar spiel about the derivation of clichés.

'He must get lonely, stuck in the flat by himself.'

'He must like it or he wouldn't do it.' But if Melissa wanted to console all the lame ducks in town, I would accede. Sausages and salad were a small price to pay for our relationship.

I decided to make an effort after all. Whatever the outcome, no one was going to blame me if the barbecue was a disaster. Melissa and I worked out the menu together. Kebabs, marinated steak and chops, the inevitable sausages. I suggested entrées; bacon rolls, paté, vol-au-vents. And a range of desserts, naturally.

'I'll pick up something from the Cheese-cake Shop. And we could make strawberry shortcake. And some of those little brandy custard tarts. Remember how you used to love cutting out the pastry?'

She smiled. 'Can you buy strawberries in April?'

'Any time, at a price.'

'Won't it be too much? Mum doesn't eat fattening food.'

'We're not just catering for her.'

Martin had sounded pleased to join the group and I was relieved. He would break up the tension I was already feeling. Roz had always been a projection on whom I could hang every characteristic I disliked. Adulterer, child-deserter, troublemaker . . . Now I would look her in the eye. Would she be the sexual, hard-drinking, chain-smoking hussy, or a cowed, beaten-down drab? Neither woman was fit to be my Melissa's mother. I was so afraid for that vulnerable little girl she'd been and for the naïve idealist she now was.

★   ★   ★

For the barbecue I wore plain jeans and a caramel angora sweater, several seasons old. Melissa's outfit certainly made up for mine. She wore a sleeveless black top dipping below the cleft of her small breasts, with a see-through maroon skirt and black boots. Her spiked-up hair and near-black lipstick exaggerated her pallor.

'How do I look?' Her gaze under pink shadowed lids was challenging.

'Like an apprentice witch. You'll freeze!'

'Well, you look like Mrs Housewife.'

'Truce? Are you ready to go?' She was chauffeuring Roz from the caravan park. I heard the car pull away and went out to greet Martin, who was carrying a bottle of fruit juice.

'Melissa's gone to pick up her mother.'

'Have you ever met her?'

I shook my head. 'This really wasn't my idea.'

'Sleeping dogs are better left to lie. You were absolutely right about that.' He sounded rueful, and I assumed he was referring to his own recent visit to the past. He helped move the tables and carry out the food until Molly started barking as Melissa arrived with her mother.

Roz wore white stretch jeans, a size too small, and a black high-necked sweater, equally figure-hugging. I had an impression of curly auburn hair and bright red lipstick. She diverted to the kennel, crouched down and fondled Molly, who at once began jumping with her dirty paws all over the white pants. Roz just laughed and brushed herself down as I prepared a fake smile of greeting. She smelled of Opium and cigarette smoke. Her hair had a rusty coarseness and her skin had a sun-baked look. Jutting breasts strained against her sweater and crimson toenails poked through her high-heeled scuffs.

'I adore dogs!' she said. 'Permanents aren't allowed them at the Park, worse luck. If I had a property like this I'd go to the RSPCA and rescue the whole crew. Dogs should be running free.'

'Unfortunately Molly's idea of freedom is to head full tilt for Brisbane. That's why she's on the chain.'

'Born under a wandering star? Sounds like me. This land's really beaut. Horses and all. Come on 'Lissa, introduce me. Who's this?' She tossed Martin a familiar smile. I expected he'd find her type a bit obvious but he sounded amused as he picked up on the banter. The sooner we got started the better. I kept busy, offering drinks and passing round the finger food. An onlooker seeing us smile and chat would have taken us for the best of friends. In fact, the small talk was a struggle. Melissa stood apart, watching us like an overseer. I maintained the hostess act and Roz had taken over Martin, who soon graduated from fruit juice to shiraz. I heard them reminisce about singers and song-writers and Martin went off to fetch his guitar. We three females stood docile as deer summoned by the stag as he played a half dozen 70s songs, the instrument cradled and his eyes flickering towards Melissa's plunging neckline. At least my dog was having a good time. She leapt and pranced, snatching titbits mid-air like a seal.

Dying to get the ordeal over with, I carried out the meat tray. Martin insisted on cooking. He stood prodding the steaks to leather while

Molly went berserk at the savoury scent. Melissa stood withdrawn and shivering near the hot plate.

'Honey,' called Roz, 'you'll catch your death.'

I had to agree. 'Yes. Go and slip on something warm,' I suggested.

Melissa turned on us both. 'I'm fine. Stop fussing.'

She stalked into the house. Of course this happy reunion was a fiasco. If she'd hoped Roz and I could meld into a single love object and erase the past, this meeting only confirmed our gulf.

'The steak's about ready,' Martin said, inspecting the singed lumps of meat. Roz took a small sausage and helped herself to salad. I did the same. Molly sat bolt upright, nose tilted, paws modestly together, as though hoping to win the school captaincy ballot. Martin topped up our glasses, then drained the second bottle of wine into his own. We'd given up all attempts to make conversation. Quite soon he gathered up his guitar and excused himself.

'Won't you stay for dessert?'

'I'm not a sweets man and I have a little job to see to. I'm starting a lad with guitar lessons. Thanks for the meal, Sara. Nice to meet you, Roz.' He shed his gentle, abstracted smile on us both.

Roz and I stood looking after him.

'Cheesecake?'

I sounded desperate and suddenly we both began to laugh.

'Want a hand to clear up?'

We carried the dishes inside.

★ ★ ★

Melissa was in her room, a CD blaring.

'Is she OK? She seemed upset.' Roz clattered plates and I was glad the Wedgwood was tucked away. 'We're still getting to know each other. It's been a long time.'

She wasn't telling me anything new. I didn't reply.

'She doesn't remember the early years. Paul and I were actually happy then. Melissa was our little love child.'

I kept on washing.

'But he turned me off in the end. Poor old Paul. You must know, you were married to him. They say boarding school's where it starts. Cruel little beasts, boys; and the teachers, some of them. I went along with the SM games. Made him happy. But I wasn't that way myself.'

'I don't discuss another person's sexuality.' I meant to sound stiff. Roz had really shocked me, because in fact we weren't mulling over common facts about our former husband. Paul had never broached that kind of sex with me. Her inroads threatened me at every turn. My stepdaughter, my dog, now the man I'd once loved and thought I knew. But it seemed Paul had never really shared himself with me. Our sexual encounters had been bland, routine. Pleasant. My mind reeled with images of Paul cringing before Roz in the gear of a dominatrix. Horrible! And Roz was laughing about it!

The music from Melissa's room had stopped and she emerged, wearing everyday jeans and jumper.

'You two seem to be getting along all right.' It sounded more like an order than an observation.

'Yes. Are you hungry?'

'Not much.'

'What about some cake before you drive your mother home?'

'Try some, Mum? Sara makes the best shortcake.' Suddenly she dropped a kiss on both our cheeks and I thought that perhaps the barbecue hadn't been such a bad idea.

After they'd gone I sat musing. You think you know a man you married and lived with for years. You share the bed, the chequebook, the funny and the tragic moments. We shared

Melissa's childhood. Yet the Paul Roz talked about was a stranger to me. I'd never understood how he chose to marry her. Given his low opinion of her mind and her morals, she seemed totally unsuited to him. Had he assumed he could safely reveal his nature to her because he felt himself to be in every other way superior? Rational Paul, plagued by urges he couldn't control? Clues came to me now . . . The way he encouraged me to splash out on a new leather handbag or high Italian boots.

Our antiseptic love life never probed the depths he must have sought with Roz. I suppose he'd shown himself and lost her. She'd tired of him. No doubt I would have, too. Poor man. Paul would be the last man to transgress society's laws or mores; and the last to deserve punishment. It was wrong of Roz to talk about him. He was entitled to his secrets. We all have them. I'd never told him about my baby. Melissa was so secretive about her mother. Martin kept his doubts and suspicions from his wife. I thought what remote lives we all lead. Perhaps we were all strangers.

7

Martin

Molly's racket drew my attention to the paddock gate. Sara was enticing the bay up the ramp of a horse float. I kept out of the way until both horses were aboard and the driver had pulled away, then wandered over.

'What's happening?'

Sara stood looking after the departing vehicle. 'The owner's going to winter them up North.' There was a wistful look about her. 'You can't help getting attached when you care for them.'

'You'll miss your morning rides.'

'I'll bring in a couple of hacks. They'll be more suitable for kids anyway.'

I remembered she'd mentioned giving riding lessons. 'Adam will be here for the Easter break. I'll see if he's interested.'

'I usually get a few bookings then. Quiet, Molly! Does her barking worry you?'

I preferred the silence of cats but diplomacy seemed called for. 'She's a bundle of energy.'

'She needs far more exercise than I give her. I'm getting a quote to fence the property. Oh well, things to do. See you.'

Sexy in the fitting jodhpurs and red checked shirt, she ruffled the dog's coat and went back to the house. She seemed to give all her affection to her animals. There was no man on the scene and she was alone at the barbecue. I'd thought about asking her out. We were both unattached and probably had a good deal in common. But I sensed the *noli me tangere* signal. Better not to get involved. I had enough complications in my life.

★ ★ ★

The DNA tests were done and paid for. It was a matter of waiting now. I was sure I'd taken the right step to clear up my doubts but Carol was still furious with me.

'Adam made a joke of it. Then he came back to me later and said, *So that explains things*. I said, *What things?* I saw tears in his eyes. *Dad's never cared about me*. Those were his exact words, Martin.'

'Of course I care.' No doubt Carol was playing up the impression of unloving father to the hilt. 'This is a totally separate issue.'

'If you say so.' She hung up the phone, leaving me riddled with guilt. Quite frankly I was dreading my son's visit, confined together in the small space of the flat. I wondered whether he and Bruce might hit it off. The boy had been for his first guitar lesson. Much of it I'd spent trying to put the battered instrument back in tune. Bruce hadn't exaggerated. It had been wrecked. I showed him my old Gibson; a flat-top I'd been lucky enough to pick up second hand in the early days.

'What's it worth?'

'On today's market, about ten thousand.'

He gaped at that. 'Why don't you sell it?'

'It's a beautiful instrument.'

'You could get something cheaper and pocket the rest.'

I felt a twinge of disappointment. That's how the young ones are.

'Let's hear that first string tune again.'

He obediently repeated the exercise, dogged rather than talented. Just a subtle thing, battling the notes rather than releasing them.

'Relax, mate! Here, like this.' But he wasn't attentive and simply repeated the same mistakes again. I felt his gaze, hungry for a word of praise.

'I'll show you a few chord shapes.' I demonstrated a couple of verses of *The Yodelling Pig*.

'That's one of your songs.'

'How do you know?'

'It's on your CD. Mum plays it sometimes. I'd like to make a CD. How many lessons would it take?'

I had to laugh. 'I thought writing was your *forte*?'

'I'm pretty good. You teach English, don't you?'

'That's right.'

'I'm entering another story competition. I'll show you if you like.'

'When it's finished, why not? How about we go over those first string notes again?'

I tried to loosen up his left-hand position. His knuckles were white with effort.

'Relax! Don't fight it. She's a gentle instrument, she needs persuasion.'

He didn't understand me. Despondent, he dumped down the guitar like a log of wood. 'I knew it was a wreck. Maybe I can buy a better one.'

It wasn't his fault. He belonged to a generation reliant on equipment. I was glad to see the time was up. Ben usually called for him on his way back from the mine.

'It's time we packed up. Your father will be waiting.'

'Thanks, Mr Ainsworth.'

'*Martin* will be fine.'

We walked down to the gate together.

Bruce stopped to pat Molly as we passed. Laughing like that, he was just an unguarded child, despite the downy chin and pimples.

'Like dogs, do you?'

'Sure. They're OK.'

'There's your Dad's ute.'

'Thanks, Martin. See ya!' He brushed off his school trousers like a junior executive and ran ahead.

* * *

I'd thought no more about Bruce, much less his chatter, when he turned up to his next lesson with a new guitar.

'I used my competition prize money, plus Mum and Dad put in some.'

I played a round of chords and handed the instrument back. The action was easy and the tone mellow. 'Very nice.' *Some* must have been several hundred dollars. He'd learned the first string notes and played them just as doggedly, his lips compressed. If he made a mistake he had a strange habit of tapping the side of his head with his knuckles. We did the second string.

'Am I doing better, Martin?'

'It's early days. Keep practising.'

'I'd like to join the school band. They get trips to Sydney.'

I said nothing. I doubted I could teach Bruce to be a musician but one thing we'd learn was patience. As he was leaving he pulled a couple of pages from his backpack and thrust them into my hand.

'Your competition entry? You realise I can't make any changes to it?'

'I've already posted it. That's just a copy. I don't need it back.'

I glanced at the heading. *An Australian Family's Day*. The dated topic surprised me. I'd found that horror, fantasy or science fiction appealed more to Bruce's age group. When he'd gone I decided to read the piece and get it over with.

We're not rich and we're not posh. Our ute's rusty. We live in a dump. In my school uniform I look like the other boys, neat and clean. Inside I'm disgusting. I don't have many friends. I have to win a scholarship to stay on at my school next year. I can't slack off. Teachers like me because I'm brainy. My parents think education is a huge deal — especially my Mum. I can get anything I want as long as I say it's educational. I could probably get a private plane.

Dad's a miner. He comes in wearing

dirty clothes and filthy work boots. He can't leave his beard alone. He sits there, rubbing it. It scrapes softly, like a dying cicada. Dad's rough. He mucks around with my little sister, Joanne. He tickles her and fools about until Mum says 'All that noise hurts my ears.' She watches and smiles. She likes to see everyone happy. But lately she's changed. She watches in a different way. 'Don't be rough, Ben. You're getting her over-excited.' So Dad laughs and swings Joanne low to the ground, and tips her up so she's hanging by her heels, all red-faced, mouth wide open. 'Ooh, aah, put me da-oown!' When Dad puts her down she swings round like a windmill, and her arms hit Dad on the legs, smack smack smack and Dad reaches down and tugs her curly hair so she squeals louder. He's right into it, down on the floor, growling like a bear, chasing her round the room. So Mum shouts at him. 'That's enough! Have your dinner. We've had ours.'

He gets his off the stove and shoves the mess on the table over so he can find a corner to sit down and eat.

★   ★   ★

Dad came to pick me up from school in the rusty ute. He parked at the school gate. I was walking out with Alastair. We're not friends, just in the same Maths class. His father drives a Porsche. He saw the ute. He scoffed, 'How's that for vintage!' So I walked straight past Dad. I wanted to strangle him when he honked the horn and I had to get in. 'Don't ever pick me up again,' I said. I felt so red in the face I thought I was having a stroke like my grandfather. Dad drove home. He didn't say anything. Just before we went in he gave me a look like his heart was broken. 'What are they doing to you, son?' he said. I didn't know an answer. 'I hate that school,' I said. 'I want to go to the State school.'

So now there's a huge argument going on later when we're supposed to be asleep. What are they fighting about? Education, naturally!

'You never managed to make anything of yourself, now you want to spoil your children's chances!' That's Mum.

'They don't belong there with those people with their Jags and Porsches!' That's Dad.

'At least they can grow up to be

respectable people, professional people with a decent life.'

'Don't give me that, Annie! You don't know what real life is.'

'Oh, don't I! It's this penny-pinching misery you give me.'

Crash! That's Dad hitting the kitchen table.

'Don't you dare get violent with me, Ben Marshall, I'll be down to the police station so quick smart — '

'That'd be right! You'd tell the cops I was the one who started the fight, just because I don't like my kids turning into bloody little snobs like you.'

'They'll have a proper education if I have to scrub the streets on my knees.'

'And I say they can get that at the State school. They'll be moved at the end of the year.'

'Never!'

Crash! That's the front door slamming. The walls shake. The ute won't start till after four goes. Then it roars away. The house is dead quiet. I look in the other room. Mum's sitting at the kitchen table. She's staring at her arm, giving it a little rub. She looks up, sees me.

'I'll see he doesn't come to the school

again,' she says. 'He doesn't belong there.'

'I don't either. I want to go to the State school.'

'Oh don't be so silly,' she says. 'Did you finish your homework?'

I shake my head.

'Then go and do it.'

I leave her, rubbing her arm. Dad's back next morning.

Everybody's quiet. Life's normal. This is the end of a day in the life of an Australian family.

★ ★ ★

I re-read the piece slowly. I wished I'd never run into Annie that fateful morning. Now I was tutoring a boy who was so torn apart he was actually naming his parents in an indictment, begging for an audience. Did he want my intervention? This piece wasn't written for any competition. The bland heading suited primary school mentality. How many similar themes had I set and marked during my early teaching years? Picnics. Trips to the beach. Christmas morning.

But Bruce's day was no picnic. Children don't write scenes like this to entertain. The family was locked in conflict. I thought of the way Ben patiently waited at the gate; how Bruce hurried away as though he didn't want me to encounter his father. I remembered Annie's passion as she said *My children will never have to struggle, the way Ben and I do.* I could see Bruce's white knuckles as he clutched the new guitar like a weapon of challenge.

I'd made a firm decision to distance myself from the Marshall family. I should never have intervened. As soon as decently possible, I'd intended to discontinue the music lessons and extricate myself from their lives. Yet the fact of the matter was that Bruce had offered me his trust. Why me? I had no idea at all. I didn't much like him, yet he'd chosen me. How could I toss his words aside and walk away?

★　★　★

The letter I'd been waiting for arrived a few days later. As soon as I saw the envelope I felt a frisson of sick anticipation. The wording of the report was brief. I stood re-reading the few sentences. DNA testing had shown Adam to be my son. There was the fact. I was glad of it, I even hoped I'd taken a step towards establishing a new relationship between us. I wonder what made me think Adam would step from the train smiling, when I went to collect him for the holidays?

So much for that little fantasy. He met me with a scowl. There was no response to my awkward hug.

'What's in the bags?'

'My stuff.'

I raised my eyebrows at the two large cases. 'A fair bit for two weeks!'

'Mum's sent a letter.' He fumbled in his pocket. I opened the envelope and read the curt note there on the wind-blasted platform.

Adam has been expelled from school. He'll give you the details. Quite frankly I've had enough. I've decided it's your turn to deal with our son and whatever issues you both need to resolve. Liz and I will be away for an indefinite period. I'll forward you an address later. Carol

Adam stood kicking his shoe against a planter box. He'd be thirteen soon. I was at a loss. I could deal with a full classroom of boys his age easier than I could my own son.

'We've got a bit of talking to do,' I said. 'And don't do that.' He stopped kicking the box. 'Let's get these bags over to the taxi.' I lifted one. I heard him trailing along behind me, scuffing the other suitcase along the ground. The sound grated on my nerves. I turned and faced him.

'Whatever your problem is, while you're with me you'll have to behave. Is that understood?'

'Sure, *Dad.*' His insolence got to me and I dumped his suitcase in the middle of the parking lot.

'Carry it yourself.' I was furious with both him and Carol. I didn't care much what her motive was for this inconsiderate, unannounced arrival. With no preparation and no warning I was stuck with Adam's full time care and education. I'd have to share my tiny flat with a surly boy whose last wish was to be with me. I strode ahead to a waiting cab. My son followed, dragging his feet, scuffing both bags along the ground.

8

Sara

Adam arrived yesterday. The poor kid sparked off a crisis! Martin turned up on my doorstep at eight o'clock to phone his ex-wife and was very angry when there was no reply to his call. She'd apparently shuffled off the boy and gone away.

'Sit down and I'll brew some coffee,' I suggested because he was so upset.

'I suppose you'll want me to move out?'

'Why would I?'

'You didn't take on my son when we signed the lease.'

'I'm sure it will work out. Perhaps Adam needs this time with you.'

'Well, *I* certainly don't need him at present.'

I held my tongue. I knew how he felt. In recent weeks I'd had a few occasions myself when I wished the past would go away. I wondered constantly about my baby, now a grown woman. And when I wasn't thinking of Shannon (not even knowing her adoptive name) I was re-living my marriage to Paul.

'You're welcome to stay on. Where's Adam now?'

'Asleep on the settee — stuff scattered everywhere. I can't see this working.'

'In what ways?'

Martin combed frantic fingers through his dark hair. 'He's been expelled. What am I supposed to do with him here? Take him to see the Aboriginal Keeping Place and historic homes?'

'Other teenagers find plenty to do. Just give it time.' I slipped crumpets into the toaster.

'I don't know how I'll handle the extra expenses. New uniforms, food, clothing. I'll have to get a new computer for him. My laptop's on its last legs.'

Did he really think material things would resolve their differences? Now he would have a chance to be a real father. Martin might be concerned with the abstract issues of parenting but he had no idea of its reality. It wasn't the time to remind him these were the same problems his ex-wife had been dealing with since their separation. He sat deep in thought while I set the table and put out margarine, jam and honey. Brewing coffee began to scent the air.

'At least I am his father,' he suddenly announced.

'The results came back? How does that make you feel?'

'A bit of a fool! I've alienated him even further, if that's possible.'

I poured two mugs of coffee. 'I'm sure it'll work out. Just give it time. There's a stretcher bed and camp mattress out in the shed. I've got an old screen, too. At least we can get him fixed up with his own space.'

The crumpets popped. I sat watching him eat, realising how long it was since I'd shared my breakfast table with a man. The moment felt domestic; I in my dressing gown, Martin unshaven. I wanted to reach out and fix his unevenly buttoned shirt. Fortunately he wasn't a mind reader. He finished eating and had a second cup of coffee.

'I really appreciate this, Sara.'

'You're welcome.' I was enjoying the feeling that he needed me.

⋆　⋆　⋆

I met Adam later. He was a good-looking lad, tall for his age, with a crop of white-blonde hair. He clearly resented everything about the new arrangements. He ignored us as Martin shifted books and magazines, assembled the stretcher and lugged in the old chest of drawers I'd emptied of its rubbish. Set up in a corner of the tiny living room, they hardly made a fashion statement.

'There's a screen stored in the rafters, Adam,' I said. 'Why don't you get it down?' I paid no attention to his scowl. His school didn't want him, his mother couldn't put up with him and his father wouldn't accept him without scientific proof. No child deserved such rejection. I smiled at him. 'Well, perhaps later,' I conceded. 'I'll bring you spare sheets and blankets, and something to hang your clothes from.'

Once the work was done, I offered to cook up pancakes for lunch. I earned a begrudging nod from Adam. Martin sounded diffident.

'You're sure we won't be in the way?'

'I've got nothing planned.'

In fact I found myself looking forward to their company. Melissa wasn't home much any more. She'd found part-time work, playing at weddings with a small musical group, and had joined forces with a flautist to go busking in the Mall. Much of her spare time she was with Roz. I suspected she was helping her mother out with money but didn't dare ask. There was a brittle tone to our brief exchanges. I'd got the message. *Keep it light!*

'What are we going to do now?' Adam said after lunch. He sounded thoroughly bored and Martin jumped on him at once.

'You'll have to learn to entertain yourself here. What do you usually do on a Sunday?'

'Muck around.'

'Then you can muck around unpacking.'

'What about going for drive?' I suggested. 'I feel like getting out.'

Really, the pair seemed incompatible as cat and dog. I could understand why Martin had wanted the genetic testing, cold-hearted though it seemed. I wondered if he'd gained in any way by the exercise. There was no sign that he felt closer to the boy. He'd said, *I just want to know*. That was, really, how I felt, if I were honest. I'd decided to try and trace my adopted daughter. In fact I'd already taken one small step and found the Adoption contact address.

I backed out the car and Molly set up her usual racket. Adam bent down and threw a length of stick at her. It may have been a playful gesture. Molly certainly thought so. But I'd be keeping a watchful eye on him.

I felt sorry for my dog, leaping and straining at her chain. Roz had prodded my conscience. It wasn't right to keep such an active animal confined, but the two fencing quotes had left me reeling.

'Be patient!' I called. 'When I get back, we'll go for a good walk together.'

105

＊　＊　＊

The drive to town was between an avenue of poplar trees, golden in the autumn light. We passed Roz's attractive caravan park; its small pond and red and yellow foliage breaking the stretch of green lawns. Armidale was pretty, nature-wise, and the cathedrals and historic buildings created a refined atmosphere. But what did it have for a twelve-year-old boy?

'What do you do in your spare time, Adam?'

'Cruise. Hang out at Timezone. Go skateboarding.'

'I think there's a ramp somewhere.' I seemed to remember one near town, adolescents swarming the concrete slopes like marauders.

My rear-vision mirror showed Martin's unsmiling profile and Adam's set face. I struggled on. 'There's the Arboretum.'

'What's that?'

'Native plants and trees, aquatic gardens. People take picnics there.'

Adam's silence conveyed utter boredom. I drove past the deserted Mall, where a Sunday afternoon may as well be midnight. I was feeling desperate.

'I know. We'll take the Heritage Drive.'

'Anywhere you think. It's all delightful.'

106

Martin was adamant.

'Where's Timezone?' Adam muttered.

'Your priority here will be schoolwork. Not skateboarding.'

I couldn't stand twenty-five kilometres of this. 'We'll go to Uralla. Thunderbolt's haunt.'

'What's that?'

'Bushranger country. You'll see.'

I didn't have much in mind to show him — just the effigy of the tubercular little robber in the museum, his cast image on horseback in the main street and his grave on the outskirts of town. Rough justice, the fact that now it was his name that attracted tourism and trade to the place he'd once held at gunpoint!

We drove in silence, until, near Rocky River, Martin asked me to detour. A kilometre along the country road he asked me to stop for a few minutes, and left us at the gate. Soon he came back with another boy, a few years older than Adam; I'd seen him carrying a guitar bag to Martin's flat.

'OK if Bruce comes with us?'

It certainly made no difference to me, and Adam was keeping mute. The boy buckled himself into the front seat. As we drove off I saw a woman wave from the veranda. Martin leaned forward.

'Bit of a surprise, mate? We're going to the museum.'

The rear vision mirror showed Adam folding his eyelids inside out. The gangly boy beside me, however, seemed quite enthusiastic. Evidently he liked the attention and I thought Martin was labouring a point, as though trying to show his son up. I had a sense that the woman on the porch was some connection from the past.

Martin seemed to read my mind. 'Bruce's mother and I were at Uni together. She'd like us to stop in for coffee later. All right?'

I nodded brusquely, thinking of my broken promise to poor Molly. How had a casual drive turned into this marathon? But I didn't want to add more fuel to this cold war. Adam was now taking imitation pot shots at the back of Bruce's head. Martin snapped a reprimand. In silence I drove on to Uralla.

★ ★ ★

McCrossins Mill was closed that weekend for renovations. The coin-in-the-slot history of Captain Thunderbolt was jammed and weeds grew on the bushranger's dismal grave. The boys hadn't spoken. Martin and I worked away at good cheer like a pair of evangelists, but by the time we stopped at Bruce's house I

108

had a headache and was determined to cut the visit short. Unfortunately Annie had other ideas. The young people went off to play some computer game while we sat and waited. Annie, who'd given me one glance, then acted as though I wasn't there, seemed to be making preparations for a party. She kneaded pastry and tested a cake while my head throbbed violently. Martin was oddly formal, as though covering some alliance he refused to acknowledge. I wondered what had passed between them. I was surprised when she told him she was looking for relief teaching work. She'd have to smarten up if she wanted a job. I could see she'd once been beautiful. Now she had a careless appearance. I doubt she'd had a haircut in ten years and the lumpy cardigan and skirt did nothing for her figure. She'd dabbed on an out-of-date frosted lipstick. She would be an ideal candidate for those makeovers lucky magazine readers win. But there was no air of luck about her.

After a long silence she turned to me. 'I suppose you work, Sara?' Even her stance was unfriendly.

'I'm self-employed.'

'Sara helps the rich get richer!'

I supposed Martin was joking. I wished he'd kept quiet.

'I give advice on superannuation, that sort of thing.' I hoped that was low-key but Annie sounded defensive.

'I'll have no call to consult you. We live day by day. The children are all that matter to us. I don't suppose you have children.'

She wanted to be rude. The days when a woman had to choose between family or career were long gone.

'I have a stepdaughter.'

'So you're married?' She seemed relieved. She must have assumed Martin and I were an item.

'Divorced.'

'Well, that's the fashion.' She cast a sideways glance at Martin, inviting him to share some joke. 'It's a better option than the Wife of Bath's.'

I sat quiet, my head thudding. Was she jealous of me because I drove a new car, wore smart clothes, ran a business? The domestic trappings of family photos and home baking didn't make her a contented woman.

She turned back to Martin. 'We bought Bruce that new guitar.'

'Annie, it would have paid to wait a while.'

'But he said you advised it. He practises an hour every day. He likes you, Martin. Perhaps he should have lessons twice a week.'

'No, no! Not necessary.'

110

Martin's reluctance was quite funny but Annie didn't react.

'Bruce is so serious. He's all or nothing.'

'A pity Adam can't take a leaf out of his book.'

'Comparisons are odious, Martin,' I said. My remark seemed to please him.

'You've taken quite a shine to my renegade, haven't you?'

Annie whipped open the oven door and slapped the cake tin on the bench.

'I'll just pop in the scones.'

At this rate we'd be here until dark. 'May I use the bathroom?' I asked, vowing that in future Martin and his son could sort out their own problems. Annie indicated a room off the back veranda. The cast-iron bath, shower recess and pull-chain lavatory were stained with age. I stayed there a few minutes, washing out a tooth mug to take my headache tablets. Why did people live like this? Anyone could brighten up surroundings with fresh paint and curtains. The utter lack of grace depressed me. Greyed plastic curtains dangled torn frills. Frayed toothbrushes and oozing bits of soap littered the window ledge. The dank smell suggested dirty laundry and wet towels.

Trying to make an effort, I was refreshing my makeup in the silvered mirror when I heard heavy footsteps outside the door. A deep voice called out, 'Anyone in there?'

I opened the door. A big, kind-looking man, wearing the dirt and overalls of a labourer, smiled at me.

'Won't offer to shake hands! I'm Ben.'

'Sara.'

'Saw the Magna. Nice car. Noticed it in your drive, when I've picked up Bruce.'

'Right. Martin's my tenant. Your wife invited us for afternoon tea.'

'She likes a bit of company. I'm just going to wash up and change.'

Inside, the old water pipes groaned and whined. Washed and smiling, Ben joined us at the table.

'Now I can do things the proper way!' He thrust out his hand and I felt his warm grip while Annie's eyes fixed on the dirt embedded under his nails. 'Nice meeting you, Sara. Martin, glad you dropped in. That your boy outside?'

'Yes. He arrived yesterday.'

'Showing him around?'

'I'm afraid it was a flop,' I said. 'Everything was closed.'

'Well, you had a nice outing anyway.' He seemed that kind of man who would be quite happy to ride along a country road, quietly absorbing the stillness. His words came

112

slowly, the way a tradesman would choose a right tool for the job.

'Call the children, Ben.' Annie was busy at the oven. 'We'll have tea now.' The cat purring around her ankles, the collie padding in search of titbits, she looked a model of domesticity. The young ones wandered in; Bruce, Adam, and a curly-headed little girl who climbed up next to her father.

'Kindy tomorrow, sweetheart?' Ben ruffled her hair.

'It's school holidays.'

'So it is.' He took several scones, wiping on margarine and jam. 'Working seven days, they all feel the same.'

'Ben, our visitors might like you to pass the scones before they're all gone.'

'I haven't eaten since breakfast. Worked straight through.'

'Pass the cake please. And elbows off the table.'

The children obeyed; but somehow I felt the remark had been meant for Ben.

The tablets were working. I longed to lie down and doze. I waited a while, then interrupted Martin and Ben's talk about antimony.

'We must be going.' I stood up decisively.

'It's been lovely meeting you,' said Annie, although we'd hardly spoken. 'While everyone's on holiday we should take a picnic to the Metz Gorge. The children will enjoy that. It's a wild place. Do you remember, Martin?'

'Vaguely.' He sounded distant.

'Oh, yes. Let's all go. What's a good day for you, Sara? Saturday week? I'll make sandwiches and cook a chicken. Sara, will you bring drinks?'

Before I knew it, the outing was a *fait accompli*. It was only on the way home that I said to Martin, 'How exactly did we let ourselves be talked into this picnic idea?'

'It would have been awkward, refusing.'

I couldn't be bothered discussing it further. Silence settled. In the rear vision mirror, I saw Adam dozing, his head against his father's shoulder. I imagined taking a drive like this with my own daughter. If I followed things through and if she was willing, we could meet. What would we talk about? What emotions would we feel? Human relationships were so complicated. I only wanted to go home, lie back in my spa bath and let my darling Molly whine and lick the bubbles from my aching shoulders.

9

Martin

The Metz Gorge was a twenty minute run past Armidale. Already the landscape had a wild, untrodden look. Ancient rocks the size of huts lay haphazardly scattered about green paddocks, reminding me of vast upheavals over aeons of time.

'You're very quiet. What are you thinking about?' Annie cast me a sideways look and, briefly, rested her hand on my knee. She'd dressed up, bright lipstick, red scarf. Her nervous energy made me edgy. I'd been feeling that way since she'd told me Ben was working and couldn't come on the picnic after all. There was something about her flushed face and bright eyes that made me think of turning down a lift, but I hadn't fancied a ride in Sara's car with the hyperactive Molly.

I decided to avoid personal conversation. 'Our insignificance in the larger scheme of things.'

'You haven't changed much, Martin!'

I ignored the note of scorn. 'Here we are, a

thousand metres above sea level, on a plateau that was once an ancient seabed. I've seen perfect little shells, millions of years old, dug out of the ground, Barraba and Bingara way.'

'Was this really an ocean?' she asked.

'Prehistoric fish swam where those cows are grazing. I'm taking Adam to the local museum to help him understand the lie of the land up here.' I was pleased to have found something we could do together.

'Bruce could go with you. Ben never does anything with the children.'

Poor bloke! The man was doing his best to support his family. If Bruce's writing was to be believed, Ben was getting very little thanks from Annie. She always was hard to stand up to. I didn't envy him, mated to this fierce lioness and her precious cubs.

'Adam's busy, we'll have to see. There's schoolwork to catch up on. And Sara's started him on riding lessons.'

'Bruce should have a decent horse,' Annie said. 'Ours is beyond riding.'

'I don't want a horse, Mum.' Bruce spoke up from the back seat.

Annie paid no attention. 'How much are the lessons?'

'Better you speak to Sara about it. She's a fine horsewoman.'

'Well, fancy that!'

I had to smile a little as she concentrated on the winding road out to the gorge.

There was nothing left of the original Metz township. Once the gold had dried up, miners had moved on. Now it was hard to conjure a time when children played hopscotch and jacks, women gossiped over backyard fences and men slaked their thirst in the hotel. The people were dead; the buildings were gone. How transient we humans are, and how unimportant our dreams and failures! I'd never taken human matters as seriously as partners wanted. Even on my wedding day, I'd known I was taking part in a cultural rite. It was much the same when Dad finally drank himself into oblivion. At his funeral service I'd listened to the eulogy (*this good citizen, this fine family man*) understanding this was how we pay lip service to the dead, but recognising nothing of the man who'd been my father. Each of our roles was small and temporary. As far as I could judge, the only truth was this reality — nature, evolving, persevering.

★ ★ ★

Sara's car was parked in a grove when we arrived. Bruce jumped out and ran off in search of Adam.

'I think I'll take a wander.' I was quick to extricate myself. I was uncomfortable that Annie had brought us to this spot. Waving to Sara and Melissa, who were unpacking baskets at the picnic tables, I strode along a bush path that opened out near the cliff edge. The boys were out on the observation platform that jutted high above the drop. I walked out to join them, instinctively gripping the safety rail as I peered down the forested walls to the river, a thread of silver far below. The view was awesome. On the far side a yellow road snaked along the base of the mountainside towards a mineshaft. I had no idea whether it was still worked these days.

'What's that?' Bruce was pointing to a string of orange balloon-like objects festooning the gorge.

'Warnings to aircraft, I think.' I gazed at the terrifying expanse of open space below. Any disoriented pilot entering that gulf would surely farewell this life! A wave of giddiness made me step back. I signalled to Adam, who was showing off, pretending to swing on the railings.

'Cut that out or you can sit in the car.'

'If you fell, you'd die,' Bruce pointed out. Adam laughed and made to climb the safety fence.

'Bloody little idiot!' I pulled him down

118

roughly, imagining a missed step, his scream, the horror of losing my son somewhere in those forested depths. I'd hurt him. He wrenched free and ran away back up the path. I sighed and turned to Bruce, who stood staring into the chasm.

'It's a long way down.' He sounded in a dream. 'Do you think anyone ever jumped?'

'I hope not!'

'If you didn't die you might get stuck in a tree. Or knock yourself out on a rock. You'd wake up hours later, all alone.'

'Come on.' I wanted to get back to Adam. 'We ought to join the others.'

'In a minute. D'you want to read a chapter of my novel?'

'Not now, Bruce.'

In a determined way he'd already pulled several folded pages from his windbreaker. He handed them to me. 'I want you to read it now.'

'I'll take it home with me.'

He disliked my tone and ran off in Adam's wake.

I was anxious to find my son. There was no sign of him back at the picnic area, where Melissa and her mother were busy spreading rugs and cloths. Annie and her daughter unpacked food and Sara placed drinks on the wooden table.

'Anyone seen Adam?'

They hadn't. I went over to Bruce, who was sitting by himself, throwing sticks for Sara's dog.

'Seen Adam anywhere?'

He shrugged. 'Did you read it?'

His persistence annoyed me. 'I told you. I'll have a look at it later. Now's not the time or place. Are you sure you didn't notice where Adam went?'

'He's up there.' In a sullen way he indicated a eucalyptus tree. Sure enough, I could just make out the shape of a hunched figure high up among the branches. Relief filled me and I strolled over, not wanting to carry on the disagreement.

'Come on, son,' I called. 'Grub's up. I wasn't angry, you know. Just afraid you'd fall.'

In slow motion he climbed down and we joined the others for the meal.

Afterwards I was about to join the others for a bush walk when Annie drew me aside. 'I have to talk to you,' she said. 'Do you remember?'

I didn't much like the sound of it. Of course I remembered. We'd made love here, passionate young people totally unaware of consequence and ending. We weren't unique, and that was long ago. I had no desire to be reminded of my youth with its inflated

120

dreams and bold ambition. Those lovers no longer existed. I was about to remind Annie of the fact when she startled me, turning the expected claim into an entirely other lane.

'It's about Bruce,' she said. 'There's something you ought to know.'

'Oh yes?' Perhaps she sensed his conflict; might even have found his writing. Yet the expression in her eyes was far from that of a concerned mother.

'Have you never wondered, Martin? I was only just pregnant when you disappeared. I talked to Mum, and she said the best thing was for me to marry Ben. Bruce is your son.'

My first thought was that she'd hatched some plan to keep me in her life. I knew Annie; she'd always been inventive with a tale to excuse our late night sorties. She must be lying. But there was an awful sort of logic to her words. We'd made love, we'd taken no precautions, I'd left, and she'd married and had the baby all in a short space of time.

I'd just unravelled my doubts about Adam; now here was a second bombshell. No, I really couldn't believe her.

'How old is Bruce, exactly?'

She told me. I tallied and found the dates matched. She'd had him eight months after I'd left Armidale.

'Ben thinks he was premature.'

121

'He doesn't know?'

'Of course not! If I'd admitted I loved you and was pregnant by you, do you really think he'd have married me?'

Here was the scenario I'd blamed on Carol, quite unjustly. It was myself who'd run away and failed to face the truth.

'You married on false pretences!'

'Don't sound so righteous, Martin. What would you have done, I wonder?'

I was feeling the helplessness of all men, who may never be certain of paternity.

'How could you keep such a secret?'

'Easily! Do you think Ben would slave his guts out to educate your son?'

I wondered if Ben had ever looked at Bruce as I'd eyed Adam? Somehow I didn't think so. He seemed a generous man, who wouldn't understand deception. I saw myself, mean and small, and hit back at Annie.

'Your whole life's been a lie!'

'How dare you judge me! It was you who left!'

At that moment I would have given anything to undo my life; to be back in Newcastle, explaining the term assignments and marking essays. I felt dizzy, then afraid, as though I'd fallen off that viewing platform and dangled helplessly above that dreadful drop. In the blink of an eye, I'd acquired a second son. Annie must have a good reason for telling me now. Clearly she didn't plan to tell Ben the truth. When she'd pushed Bruce on to me, I'd taken it as the act of a doting mother who wanted payback because I'd hurt her once. Once! Now I understood that one mistake had turned into a life of unhappiness. The music lessons were her way of linking Bruce to me. She must want something. Money? Responsibilities she'd decided I should carry? I had to know.

'Annie, why now? Why tell me now?'

I was prepared for anger, blame, vindictiveness. Instead she covered her face with her hands in a gesture of pure grief. Tears ran down her face.

'You don't know, Martin. Have you any idea what it's like to marry the wrong person and realise you're tied to him? You feel half-alive. You just keep going, day after day, guilty, always acting, never saying what you really feel. Poor Ben. It's not his fault. And now I can't stand the sight of him.' Her eyes were pleading. 'I just need to be honest at last.'

And I could only think *Poor Annie!* In spite of the arguments and conflicts that led up to my divorce, I'd never thought of Carol as 'the wrong person'. Wrong people together, perhaps, but our joint life began with the sincere hopes and promises of any happy wedding day. We'd been such innocents, all of us. It was all so long ago. Compared to Annie, I'd got off scot-free. I did owe her something. But what could I offer her? This was Annie's life; not ours.

'Can you give me some time? This is a total shock. I don't know what to say.'

She nodded. 'I'm glad it's out. I know you like Bruce. He doesn't seem to be a popular boy. He appreciates the interest you take in him. He likes you. Perhaps he instinctively senses your connection.'

I doubted that. In fact it was the last thing I wanted. I hadn't taken much of a shine to him. My vision of a peaceful retreat with my book of songs and my guitar had become a joke. My days were taken over by a sulky adolescent with a TV habit and smelly sneakers. I certainly had no room in my life for another son.

'Swear you won't ever tell Ben about this?'

I was happy to agree. Ben was a big man; the sort who settled matters with his fists, perhaps.

A thought struck me. 'Does your father know?' I was remembering Douglas's strange reference to a bastard son.

'No. I only told Mum. She might have hinted. But we agreed it was better kept a secret.'

Like mother, like daughter. So Nina wasn't just a sweet old lady. I had no right to judge. I was as fine a liar as anyone, when necessary. The others were straggling back towards us. Annie quickly brushed the tears from her cheeks and resumed her maternal role, as Joanne had taken a tumble and skinned her knees. I survived the rest of the picnic in a quiet daze, wishing all this might be an hallucination.

Bruce sidled over.

'Did you read it yet?'

'I told you, Bruce. No.' My irritation seemed to pass him by.

'I think you'll be impressed. It's pretty good. I'd like to be a famous writer. When it's finished I'm going to send it to a publisher.'

'Good luck!' Was this gangling boy mine? More genetic testing could decide but I knew, deep down, that Annie was telling the truth. Bruce was my replica; clever, unpopular at school, obsessed with fame and glory. Why are our own traits so unlikeable in others? When it was time to pack up I suggested returning in Sara's car. This time, suffering Molly's hot breath and shedding coat was vastly preferable to any more intimacies with Annie.

★ ★ ★

That night the sounds of gunshots and screaming tyres filled the small flat. Too preoccupied to be bothered with rules, I'd agreed that Adam could stay up and watch some action movie. In bed, I lay reflecting on the mayhem Annie had dropped into my life. I had absolutely no idea what to do next.

In the end I picked up Bruce's wretched story. He was persistent; I'd get no peace until I'd offered some comment. Smiling at the melodramatic heading, I began to skim, then read again, more slowly, and with a growing unease.

FATEFUL STEPS. By Bruce Marshall.

CHAPTER ONE

'See me after class,' Mr Campbell told Tony, who wondered if he was in trouble for something. He'd skipped a bit of research on that last assignment. As he waited by the window, he could see boys straggling across the smooth green lawns below. The old red brick school looked warm in the sunlight. It was the kind of building he'd only seen in books; like an old English castle without the moat. From up above the boys could be soldiers in uniform, preparing for war.

But no, he wasn't in trouble. He had an A+ again. Campbell smiled as he handed back the work. 'Keep it up and you'll get that scholarship next year,' he said. Talk about the scholarship made Tony feel a bit sick so he tried not to think about it as a rule. Money was short and the school fees were very expensive. His parents did the best they could but there were other children to educate and it was expected that Tony would earn a free place at the school next year. He was supposed to be clever, but so were a lot of the others who would be sitting the exam. If he didn't win, he didn't know what he would do. As he looked down at the lawns again, the thought came into his mind that he could just open the window and step out. He wondered how much it would hurt, hitting the ground from up that high, and whether the fall would be enough to kill him or just injure him. He wouldn't want to be a cripple in a wheelchair. His classmates were always laughing at freaks of one kind or another.

'You can go now,' Campbell told him. 'I just wanted to give you a word of credit for your extra effort.'

Extra effort! Campbell didn't know much! If he could see Tony at home, switched on to the Internet, browsing weird sites and gaping at the things people talked about in the chat rooms . . . It was hard to study. He felt like his head was stuffed with wet newspaper. Foggy and dead. He couldn't think, though answers popped out of his mouth or off his pen as though a robot managed his life.

Tony went downstairs, hoping most of the boys had gone by now. His heart sank when he saw Blake and his mates standing near the gate. Oh no! The last thing he wanted was for that lot to see him being picked up in his father's rusty old truck, covered in dust from the dirt road out to the mine. He thought he could hang around the side until the others had gone, but then he saw the truck, parked right there at the front gate in full view of everyone. Blake nudged Keith and laughed. They'd spotted him. They knew it was his father. Tony wished now he had jumped out that window.

'Hey, Henshaw! That guy's waving to you! Must be going to the vintage rally! Better hurry up if you want to make it home before dark . . . Might have a breakdown on the way!'

They all cracked up as Tony walked past and slammed the pickup door.

'Hi son!' his father said, revving up so smoke burst out the exhaust and blew in through the open window. He was wearing his miner's overalls and looked filthy. 'How was school?'

'Don't ever pick me up at school again!' Tony said angrily. He felt sick with humiliation. Everybody knew Blake's father drove real vintage cars, as well as a BMW. All the parents had money and new cars and went overseas. He hated them and he hated himself. His father was silent, most of the way home. He only spoke to Tony as he parked in their run-down yard, and his voice sounded terribly sad.

'What are they doing to you, son?' was all he said.

Tony didn't answer. He didn't know what to say.

'I'd rather go to the State school,' he said, but it wasn't really true. He didn't want to be an ordinary kid at an ordinary school and he didn't fit in with rich kids. He didn't belong anywhere. He thought of himself lying quiet and peaceful on the school lawn. Dead or not, everybody would be fussing round, the ambulance siren would be sounding and he would never have to be a winner or face the bullies again.

'I'm going in, Dad,' was all he said. 'I've got a pile of homework to do.'

END OF CHAPTER

I laid the pages down. They were the same theme re-worked but the mediocre writing didn't matter. Something was very wrong. Was Bruce contemplating suicide? These things happened. I could remember two separate events in my teaching career where boys had died. One, who had lost a leg in a motor accident, had gone into the bush with a bottle of his mother's sedatives. The other, a boy who knew he was gay, had drowned in suspicious circumstances. Both times I'd felt that terrible sense of wasted young life. I wished I could have helped the victims see past their present despair.

I could forget any ideas I had about avoiding the Marshalls. I had to talk to Annie and her son as soon as I could.

10

Sara

After that day out with Martin and Adam, I came to a decision and sent off a letter to the adoption agency. I didn't expect anything would come of it and felt very uncertain when they sent back registration forms and a letter stating they had information regarding my enquiry. I filled out the papers at once and returned them by next-day delivery. The people down in Sydney were efficient. Along with the phone bill, two charity appeals and a letter for Melissa, addressed in Paul's handwriting, their communication arrived within the week. They said my daughter had registered with them some time ago. She didn't want to make contact with me. However, in the event that I ever filed an enquiry, she wished me to be informed that she had a blood coagulation disorder called thrombophilia. The condition is hereditary and as such natural parents should be tested.

I don't know how many times I re-read those meagre lines. After the hopes I'd built up, they seemed so cold and formal. *Your daughter does not seek contact with you.* The only intimacy I would ever know with her was that, perhaps, we both carried a damaged gene. I'd never heard of thrombophilia and, to date, had no evidence that there was anything wrong with my blood. My hand was shaking as I read the lines yet again, looking for some other, tiny shred of hope. *Your daughter does not seek contact with you.*

I dialled the Internet, found *Health* and ran a search. There were plenty of references to scan. The condition, also called Factor Five Leiden, was apparently present in 3-7% of the population in America and Europe. There was an increased risk of blood clots, strokes and heart attacks. A simple blood test could identify the disorder. I was taking a copy of the information when Melissa arrived. She had a look over my shoulder.

'Why are you printing that out?'

'Just interested.' I didn't want to tell her yet. 'Coffee?'

'Please. Don't switch off. I want to run a search on breast implants. Mum's have to be taken out. One's infected.'

Typical, I thought. Melissa seemed to be completely caught up in her mother's life. I'd always seen Roz as a bit of a vampire. Sharing her difficulties came only too easily to her. It wasn't my way at all.

By the time the coffee was brewed, Melissa had printed out several pages of gruesome images. The sight of dank, mould-infested bags and seeping wounds made me shudder. As well, she had pages on support groups and compensation claims.

'When's Roz having surgery?'

'She's on a waiting list. Mum can't afford health insurance.'

I skimmed the printed sheet she'd dropped on the table. *Malpractice suits, gross negligence, misrepresentation* . . . lawyers must be having a field day.

'I can't think why anyone would have that kind of plastic surgery,' I said.

'No one told her this could happen. She just wants it fixed.'

I picked up Paul's letter. 'This came for you.'

She opened the envelope, looking pleased as she pocketed two $50 notes. She skimmed the sheet then passed it to me. Paul's tiny, meticulous script was the same but his usual whimsy was absent.

'It doesn't sound like him.' She must have asked him for money. He said he was sorry he couldn't send more, but his position at the university was under review, his roof had to be replaced, and he'd had a fall and was scheduled for a knee reconstruction any day. The flatness of his writing concerned me. I reminded myself it was nothing to do with me. Now he had a separate existence; another woman to talk to about his choices and his worries. He knew nothing about my current life. Melissa was the one link between us now.

'Why don't you drop him a line? He sounds a bit down.'

Melissa didn't seem concerned. 'At worst, he'll get a fat redundancy package. And I'll bet he's got the best of specialists and private hospitals.'

Not like poor Mum! How long was this partisanship going to go on? I didn't need to be a mind reader to know where Melissa's loyalty and a good bit of her money went these days. I wished she would spend that much energy thinking about her own future.

★　★　★

Molly at my feet, I was home alone that night, skimming the figures in the property trust's report, when there was a tap at my door. It was Martin. I was surprised. He kept to himself in the evenings. Turned out he'd had a run-in with Adam. The boy started at his new school a few weeks ago and was already in trouble. Martin was absolutely furious. He'd given Adam the third degree and found out why his ex-wife had given up on the boy.

'I found out what's been going on. An appalling list! Shop-lifting, graffiti, vandalism ... I've warned him, if he doesn't apply himself to his schoolwork, he'll be straight into the strictest boarding school I can find. I won't tolerate this!'

The cool, calm man had disappeared. I could understand his anger but he was raving. Martin was clearly a lot more emotional than he let on. I felt sorry for Adam! Martin's strict rules must be his way of keeping control of himself. No wonder he had lapses.

'God, I need a drink!'

I couldn't refuse. 'I only have wine. Red or white?'

I could tell he didn't care if I poured home brew or hooch. He emptied his glass at one gulp. Gradually he calmed down. Resuming his everyday manner, he picked up the report lying on my coffee table and riffled the pages.

'Is this how you spend your evenings, Sara?'

'Not always. I'm reviewing a client's portfolio. This company has a new fund manager.'

He dropped the report back on the table.

I'd gathered he had little interest in finance. Plenty of intelligent men and women take a perverse pride in remaining financially illiterate and nothing about Martin seemed established. He was educated and artistic, yet lacked possessions and relationships. He made me curious.

'Do you have any plans? Goals?' I asked.

He leaned back on my leather sofa cushions and smiled at me. 'Isn't that a rather New Age question?'

So he wanted to spar. 'I think it's a sensible question.' And I returned the smile.

'You seem very sorted out,' he suggested.

'I may seem like that. But you don't really know me, do you?'

'Don't I? What don't I know?'

Persuasive, he moved closer to me. I wanted to talk to someone. I blurted out the story of the adoption and my enquiry. Telling him about the letter I'd received was painful. I'd taken a huge emotional risk and lost. As an afterthought, I mentioned the medical situation.

'That must be a worry,' he said, as though the fact that my daughter didn't want to know me was a side issue.

'I couldn't care less about it! My child doesn't want to meet me. That's what's upsetting!'

136

I was on the edge of tears. Molly licked my hand. Martin refilled his glass and stood looking thoughtful.

'May I read the letter?'

I passed it to him and he scanned the contents.

'They don't say how long ago the girl sent them this information.'

'No.'

'People do change their minds. She might have a different perspective now. Why not try again?'

He was trying to cheer me up. My hopes flared. He could be right.

'I suppose I could ask the agency to approach her.'

'She can only say no.'

I didn't want to consider that, and changed the subject. 'What does Adam feel about his riding lessons? Does he enjoy them?'

'No idea. He doesn't say.'

'Don't you ask?' Poor kid! Who could guess what went on in his young head? Adam was often surly and he seemed a bit afraid of the horses, but he paid attention whenever I gave him instruction.

'Fact is, Sara, I need to find some extra income. I hadn't budgeted on Adam.'

I couldn't understand a parent talking like this, as though his son was just another bill to pay. His attitude was almost as haphazard as Roz's. Every object in this room I'd handpicked. I'd earned proper qualifications to do a responsible job. I knew where I'd be next week, next year. Insurances, investments and savings protected me. And here was a father unprepared for the expenses of his only child.

'What sort of work are you looking for?'

'I saw a tour company's advertising to have some brochures written up. I might give them a try. Worst case, I can be a pizza delivery man.'

'You're not allowed to drive.'

'What a pragmatic woman you are!'

An atmosphere was growing between us. We'd both opened up and shared our deepest concerns.

'Sara?' He moved closer to me. I felt his arm reach around me. I turned to him and buried my face against his shoulder. He smelt nice. His fingers gently caressed my hair. It was cosy; the heater glowing, Molly's dreaming whuffs and whickers punctuating the silence.

'Do you give lessons in success?' he murmured.

'What do you mean?'

'My life's a total mess. Look at me! I've been in court, and I'm a rotten father. What's your secret?'

My outer life might seem in order but I was far from sorted out.

'Actually, we're both the same. I'm searching for my daughter. You need to reach your son.'

'I'm not sure I can reach Adam. I don't know how to guide him.'

He'd stopped caressing me. I moved closer, calling his attention back to me. We'd said enough. He was here, and I felt lonely and needy. His fingers strayed across my breasts. Molly stirred, stretched and lay back with a heavy sigh. Behind me, Martin reached across and turned off the lamp.

★   ★   ★

In the morning I opened the curtains and lay idly stroking Molly while I reviewed my plans for the day. I had a GST seminar on at ten, then two business meetings. I scratched Molly's belly and she rolled onto her back, paws sticking up, grinning in her look of idiot contentment. I didn't feel my usual impulse to scribble in my diary. Yesterday's extremes had passed and I was left in submissive peace. I wasn't ready to think about Martin, and whether last night had been anything more than an unplanned interlude. I think we were both surprised. The physical contact was

139

pleasurable, but we'd said goodnight on a friendly rather than intimate note.

I hadn't made up my mind about asking the agency for further details, but the thrombophilia information was another matter. I re-read the printouts about Factor Five Leiden. They were a dreary prospect of blood clots, miscarriage, gall bladder dysfunction, eclampsia, stroke or heart attack. I decided to make an appointment for a test as soon as possible. It was a strange feeling to accommodate this possible diagnosis. In the shower I seemed to feel breathless. I noticed a small red mark on my leg and wondered if it might be the first indication of a clot. I considered an omelette, remembered eggs were high in cholesterol and went for muesli instead. Over breakfast I sat reflecting that in the past day I'd lost a daughter, gained a lover and could possibly drop dead of a disease I'd never heard of. And Martin thought I was sorted out! I went to dress for work, grateful for the cut and dried world of my profession. At the seminar, I pinned on my registration tag and joined a group of colleagues to discuss the facts and figures of the business world.

11

Martin

Sex with Sara was the last thing on my mind when I went over to her place to air my frustration with Adam. I'd gone on impulse, noting that her lights were on and that I needed to put space between my son and myself.

'Where's dinner?' Adam whined when I told him I was going out.

'Get your own,' was all I could trust myself to say as I snatched a pullover and went out into the chilly night. My knocking roused Molly, who recognised me and stopped her racket when Sara opened the door. She was wearing a housecoat thing and her hair was damp.

'I've just got out of the bath,' she said.

'Sorry to intrude. Is it too late to talk?' My voice felt shaky from the row I'd had with Adam. Sara invited me in and I told her the gist of what had happened. Perhaps it was her manner, or the calm orderliness of her home; slowly I felt my rage changing to a more rational frame of mind, while she commiserated on the trials of adolescents.

She poured a couple of wines and we settled companionably on the sofa. The room was warm, with a gas heater replacing the old fireplace and a leather lounge suite arranged around the entertainment unit, as I'd heard them called. The pictures, of the style stocked by furnishing stores, seemed colour-matched to the rest of the set-up. Staring at the darting flames behind the glass, I appreciated the blandness of it all. Nothing too haphazard could last long in such a setting.

'So what exactly happened tonight?' She was smiling a little, as though used to calming hysterical men. I told her about the note I'd received from the school. I'd cross-examined Adam and had finally found out why he'd been expelled. He turned on the tears but I was having none of that. I left him to think over what I'd said about boarding school. I could tell Sara thought I had over-reacted but a woman wouldn't see that his long-term welfare mattered more to me than a few tears.

As the alcohol eased into my system I chose to set aside the subject of my errant son. I picked up a business report lying on the table. Glossy photographs. Graphs. The mighty dollar.

'Is this how you spend your evenings, Sara?'

142

'I have to review a client's portfolio this week.'

I sat facing a forgettable picture of magnolias, wondering how people like Sara manage to conduct such orderly lives. Spotless house, designer clothes, fingernails never a chip. What was wrong with me?

'Any plans? Goals?' she asked, as though she read my mind.

I laughed. I'd glanced through those New Age books that suggested I could have it all, I only needed to say a few affirmations. Was that what she was getting at?

In fact, my only immediate goals were, 1, to have another drink and 2, to discover the flesh and blood Sara who was so pleasantly distracting me from a fairly horrible evening. It had been a fair while since I'd sat chatting to an attractive woman in her night attire. I moved a little closer.

'Tell me about your goals instead.'

'I'm not sure. Today I received some bad news.'

She began to tell me about a baby that she'd given up for adoption when she was young. 'I've been thinking about her recently.'

I could see that even talking about the child distressed her. She'd decided to make enquiries. Apparently the answer was negative. She was sitting so that the front of her

143

gown parted, but it wasn't the time. I could see she was on the verge of crying.

'She doesn't want to meet me. She has some hereditary blood disorder and passed the information on, that's all.'

She looked quite bereft. I could see it would be very unpleasant to hear of a medical condition in such an impersonal way. Wine wasn't my drink of choice, but there was nothing else around. I refilled the empty glasses and stood looking down at her. It struck me that the daughter may well have filed her information years earlier. She might have had a change of heart. Would she have bothered to contact the agency at all, if her mother really meant nothing to her?

I put the suggestion to Sara, who, without the efficient manner, was looking up at me appealingly. She perked up at once. 'I'll think about it,' she said. 'You could be right.'

She looked very pretty sitting there in the lamp light, the dog lying at her bare feet with their little polished nails.

★ ★ ★

I sat down close to her and pressed her shoulders gently. She didn't resist; just buried her face against me while I stroked her hair and let her soft curves and sweet smell soak

144

into my senses. She moved in a way that felt inviting. She didn't resist when I began to caress her breasts. It was time to dim the light; rather to my amusement, Molly removed herself to a discreet distance and lay down with a heavy sigh.

★　★　★

I went back to my flat around midnight. A full moon shed cold light on trees and fence posts, and foliage swayed and rustled in the wind. The kennel remained deserted; Molly by now was no doubt ensconced beside or on Sara's bed. I felt pleasurably relaxed, if surprised with the evening's outcome. Well, we were adults, after all.

Adam was sound asleep. I pulled the covers over him. We'd have to begin again, with clear rules and boundaries understood. I was willing to make an effort. I knew I wasn't much of an example to him. He must have wondered why I wasn't driving. It was only a matter of time before he found out why I'd lost my licence. *Like father, like son?* Did Adam rile me so much because he mirrored my own faults? My good resolutions always failed. I might have proved the blood connection, but it had done nothing for our relationship so far. He seemed bent on throwing away his options. A good part of my lecture had concerned consequences and the risks he was taking with his future. If Adam understood anything I'd said he gave no sign. I was just another tedious stranger, telling him what to do.

In bed, I lay going over the day's events. In hindsight, I wasn't sure I'd been wise to go over to Sara's. The landlady/tenant equation worked well; I hoped she wouldn't read more into that other outcome than I'd intended. Sara was a thoroughly nice woman and she certainly didn't need the kind of trouble I tended to bring to relationships. Hopefully, in the morning, she'd see things in the same light.

My mind turned to Annie. I knew I had to see her soon. She was waiting to hear what I was going to do about Bruce and I had to air my own concerns about the boy. I wasn't looking forward to any of it. The Marshall family's bitter conflict was the stuff of a classic novel. As much as the Morels or Jude the Obscure, they seemed doomed by class divisions. The son was the rope in his parents' tug of war. Even if he managed to fulfil their hopes, would he thank them or reject them? I seemed to toss and turn for hours, mulling over problems. I had to pull up my socks as a father, if we were to avoid repetitions of the angry scene with Adam. As for the Marshalls, I wished I'd never set eyes on them.

The evening with Sara should have soothed me to sleep. Yet when I finally drifted off, it was Annie who came to me, hair streaming, lips warm, her clasp as possessive as when she used to be my love.

★　★　★

'How do you like the riding lessons?' I asked next morning, as though Adam and I were the most civil of flatmates. He gave me a wary look.

'Why?'

'Sara was asking if you plan to continue.'

'Maybe.'

'Have some toast,' I said. 'We'll jack it up after school. I'll walk along with you this morning.'

He was enrolled at the government co-ed school in Faulkner Street. Until I could sort out the rift with Carol, private education wasn't an option. My funds were in a sorry state and I intended to look around town for part-time work. Thinking of Bruce's recent writings, I left Adam to make his own way past the school entrance and went on to town. I had a few other ideas. One involved writing brochures for a local travel agency. I'd seen a news item, which said they wanted to expand beyond the usual wildflower bus tours. Surely, in a University City like Armidale, there would be a market for a literary tour? Offhand, I could think of Dorothea McKellar at Gunnedah, Henry Kendall at Kendall, and Lawson, down Mudgee way. And there were bound to be others. I planned to drop in to the library when it opened and see what research turned up.

Meanwhile I was happy to stroll. The shops were starting to open their doors and I amused myself inspecting the latest fashions and hi-tech gadgets. I soon tired of that and, drawn by rolling lawns and soaring spires, I wandered to a square bounded by several churches. It was many years since I'd been inside a Catholic church. Surprisingly, the large door was unlocked. Plaster effigies were the only human forms inside. I sat for a few minutes, unable to imagine my life ruled by a religious faith. I soon became bored and strolled across the road towards a small park. Shade trees cast broad shadows, gloomy in winter light. Memorials were spaced here and there. I read the inscription on one. *Si monumentum requiris circumspice*. Not a bad epitaph. It referred to the work of Brother Francis Gatti, who had loved trees and left this legacy. Another plaque listed fallen soldiers from the district. I'd been lucky, escaping the nets of conscription and war. What monument could I claim, if I were to drop dead today? Only my son. It was high time I found a way to help him pull his life into shape.

Back at the Mall, I was taking a coffee break when I had an unpleasant shock. At the back of the café's dim interior, I recognised Annie's mother. She was deep in conversation with a silver-haired man and it was plain they weren't just casual friends. As I watched, the man took Nina's hand and raised it to his lips. I saw her expression change to a look of yielding love.

As quickly as possible I downed the coffee, paid and walked out. The woman had found herself a lover! Why was I so surprised? I was hardly a model for conventional behaviour. Yet I'd only ever considered Nina as Annie's mother and the wife of domineering Douglas. I had an inkling of how disorienting it must have been for Adam when Carol and I announced that we no longer loved each other and were going to live separate lives. Somehow Nina, in her sixties, had the spirit to defy conventions. I don't know that I approved. Her life had probably known a lot more duty than joy. Even so, she was running quite a risk in a small community like Armidale. I'd never liked Douglas much, but it was his crippled body I pitied as I walked on up the hill. I didn't want any more secrets in my life, but this was one I'd have to keep from Annie.

I'd lost the drive to present myself as a keen job prospect. Glad to distract myself in the black and white world of biographical data, I turned in to the library. But the episode in the coffee shop wouldn't leave me alone. Nina was an attractive woman, for her age. Her admirer clearly thought so. I could understand a discreet fling but I'd seen the look on Nina's face. Women simply couldn't separate sex from love. That little confusion had wrecked every relationship I'd had in the past ten years. Nina wasn't a fool. She must know that, fair or otherwise, her place was pushing Douglas's wheelchair. My thoughts wandered to the previous night and I decided I'd acted on foolish impulse. Was it possible Sara's eyes would stare at me with that same besotted glitter?

But she seemed quite natural when I went over later to pay the rent. We spoke about Adam's riding lessons and I told her I'd made a start on job-hunting. There was no hint of involvement. A sensible woman, evidently.

12

Sara

When Paul phoned, I was expecting a client to confirm an appointment and was taken completely off guard. He was looking for Melissa and I said she was staying the night with Roz. There was a pause, loaded with pasts we'd spent together and apart.

'Melissa had your letter,' I said. 'She tells me you need surgery. How did you injure yourself?'

'I had a fall. So how are things with you?'

'I'm planning a trip. I hear you have changes at work.'

'Yes. Cutbacks.'

'Something will turn up.' I wished I could feel more sympathetic. Work had used up the best part of Paul during our married years together.

'It doesn't look promising. Would you give Melissa a message? Just tell her I love her, and I'm sorry.'

I supposed he meant about the money he'd sent. As a maintenance payment, it had been downright mean.

'Of course.'

'Thanks. I appreciate the way you've looked after her. Take care.'

'I will. And you, Paul.'

★　★　★

Brief as it was, the call left me unsettled. The trite exchange had touched on fissures of resentment and anger. I could remember his set expression, that day seven years ago, as he'd picked up his suitcase and walked out to the car. I'd watched him go, feeling the shock of a moment when your life is changing for ever.

I was in the grip of the past. Apart from Paul, there was the issue of the adoption. I'd been back to the agency, hoping Martin was right in suggesting my daughter might have had a change of heart. That train of thought had brought up my own problems with my mother, who was senile. I hadn't been to see her for a full year. I'd made a diary entry at the time. Riffling old pages, I found it, dated May 1999, and read it slowly.

I've come to a decision. I'm not going to see Mum again. It's too painful and it won't make any difference to her. She's forgotten who I am. I should say,

I've been erased from her memory 99%, but I'd swear there's something still nudging her because she grows restless when I mention Dad, or anything about our home, or even my present job. She covers up her memory deficit with a sort of patter.

A few vague phrases. Fancy that! My word! I suppose that's right! All delivered unconvincingly as though beneath these social banalities she's desperately sifting through her mind for material that's turned to dust now. Sometimes she starts to cry Sometimes she wants to walk around but then can't remember where she is or where she planned to go. Then she stops dead in the middle of the corridor and gives me this odd look as though I've deliberately lured her on a wild goose chase. Today was one of those days when she sat staring into space, saying nothing for minutes on end. Finally as I stood up and said, Mum, I've got to go now, she looked at me blankly and said, politely, It was nice to meet you, dear, in the tone she used to use to Jehovah's Witnesses or travelling salesmen at our front door. When she'd got rid of them

153

and closed the door she would sigh with relief and say to me, Thank the Lord, I thought they'd never go!

I never understood before how hard it is when the one person you've known all your life, your own mother, looks through you as though you never existed. Mum's whole life has been erased. She hardly seems aware of her present condition and there's certainly no future to look forward to. Senility leaves you with a body but takes everything that makes you individual. It's a cruel disorder. I hope I never get it. I've decided I'm going to remember her as she used to be; not as she is, with no dignity, no personality and no love left for anyone.

That made perfect sense to me when I wrote it. Perhaps I was only trying to avoid pain. I knew now it wasn't possible to chop out the parts of life that didn't go by the book. My daughter might feel just as I did. I couldn't do much about that but at least I could accept my own mother, however she was now.

★ ★ ★

154

So I went to see her. She was housed in a private hospital whose grounds created the illusion of a high-class family residence. Once inside, it was clearly a medical facility. My mother had been moved out of her carpeted front room to a different level of care (she was wandering, the staff said). They showed me through a locked door and along a linoleum-covered passage. Each alcove opened onto an idle old woman, propped in bed or tucked under rugs in a chair, staring at nothing. There was a smell of disguised urine and stale cooking. My mother was alone in her cell-like bedroom, a strap like a seat belt round her middle and a tray on wheels to her left side. Its formica surface was stained with a puddle of tea that had spilled from the spouted cup.

'Here's your daughter!' The nurse spoke in that over-loud, cheery tone one would never dream of using to an equal. My mother looked up vaguely. Crumbs of wet biscuit stuck to her mouth and dotted her pink cardigan. Her perm had grown out long ago and now her sparse hair stuck up like a cockatoo's comb. Several long white hairs curled from her chin.

'Hello dear,' she said. 'Home early from school?'

'Yes,' the nurse agreed. 'She's come to tell you all about her day.'

155

I was horrified by this nonsense, and because Mum had an inkling of who I was. She might remember I hadn't been near her for a full year.

'She didn't recognise me at all, last time I was here,' I excused myself. 'My visits were upsetting her. They said the disease only got worse as time passed.'

'She hasn't fretted. They have an occasional lucid moment, that's all.' The nurse flashed a professional face washer around my mother's face, dabbed the cardigan, and mopped up the tray with a paper towel.

Once she'd left, I gazed doubtfully into my mother's eyes. As if to prove the nurse right and ease my guilt, she looked away, tapping and humming an old nursery rhyme, over and over. *Polly put the kettle on . . . Polly put the kettle on . . . Polly put the kettle on . . .* her taps growing louder and more rhythmic. *1234567. 1234567.*

'How are you?' I ventured. She didn't respond. Surely this was a mistake. I just couldn't connect my fastidious mother with this screwball old lady in grubby clothes and bedraggled slippers. *1234567. 1234567.* Eventually, she tired of the banging and stopped.

'Well Mary! Would you like a biscuit?'

'I'm Sara.' I couldn't let go of reality; it was

so precious, and so contradicted here. Everybody, staff and patient alike, was apparently engaged in some grotesque charade.

'Have you come to play with Sara?'

'I *am* Sara!' I pulled up her chin and made her look me full in the face. 'I am your daughter, Sara. I'm grown up now, and you are in hospital.'

'Sara. That's right. She's in the yard, playing on the swing. Run along now, I've got work to do.' She yawned and her head drooped.

While she drowsed I checked her drawers and cupboard, noting the shabby look of singlets and pants. A couple of family photos smiled out from the dressing-table top but the rest of her personal belongings had presumably been packed away in storage. I was done in a few minutes; she owned so little.

There was little point in staying now. I picked up my bag and lightly dropped a kiss on her sagging head.

'Happy dreams,' she murmured, as she used to say to me every night.

I went to find the nurse in charge. 'I'll be calling for my mother next Saturday. I want to take her out for a few hours.'

'You know she's incontinent now?'

157

'I'll manage. I'm sure you can fit her out appropriately.'

'We can try. We'll get her ready for pick-up after lunch.'

My mother had come to this; a piece of furniture, scheduled for delivery. 'She was a high-school teacher, you know,' I said.

The sister nodded. 'Age is no respecter of professions. We have an airline pilot in the men's wing.' Our eyes met; I the accountant, she the nurse.

'I'll be here at half past one.' I escaped to the fresh air of the normal world.

★   ★   ★

As Saturday approached I began to worry. Eventually I took my problem to Martin and told him about my mother's condition, keeping to myself visions of a mad old lady trying to leap from the moving car.

'Could you possibly come with me when I collect her?' This felt awkward. 'I'm not sure how she'll respond to the drive.'

He seemed hesitant. 'What time?'

'One-thirty.' I wished I hadn't asked.

'I think I can make it. Bruce and Adam are going to the movies after lunch.'

'You don't mind?' I didn't like asking favours.

'Not a bit. We must get together again soon, Sara.'

'Yes, we must.' I smiled and walked briskly back to the house. I hadn't figured out what that night was all about and wasn't sure if it should be repeated. Martin was a nice man but, if I'd been looking for a lover, I doubt I'd have picked him. There was the drinking history and the financial problems, and he would be going back to Newcastle in a few months' time. Nipping our liaison in the bud was the sensible course. We weren't a couple of teenagers in love.

★　★　★

I rang the doctor on Friday but my results weren't back. Saturday was busy; I planned to prepare a special afternoon tea for Mum but didn't want to cancel Adam's riding lesson. Bruce arrived mid-morning and stood by, listening while I showed Adam how to use the hoof pick and explained the importance of regular cleaning between the farrier's visits. Adam was trotting nicely now and had lost the attitude of bravado that probably covered up a natural fear of falling off. When we'd finished the lesson I asked Bruce if he could ride. He shook his head.

'Want a quick turn around the paddock?'

159

He looked doubtful. Adam, beaming down from the saddle, urged him on. 'It's heaps good fun!'

I patted his knee, pleased to hear those words. 'You're doing really well. Soon we'll have you cantering.' The horse sidestepped as Adam dismounted and Bruce hopped nervously out of the way.

'I'll stick with my guitar, thanks all the same.'

I left the boys and went in to get ready for Mum's visit, wondering if she would have any recollection of the house. Of course she'd been here often when I was with Paul. I think her mental condition was developing even then. I didn't see it. She used to lose things, waste money, take quite irrational dislikes to old friends, but I just put it down to general symptoms of ageing. How many times did I have to bite back my impatience as I repeated the same information over and over! *I told you that!* It was years before I understood she couldn't handle her own affairs any more. I was able to take over her financial management and we tried home help and various social services. Then she had the house fire (not too serious, fortunately) and not long afterwards the falls started. Twice she ended up in hospital. The rest home was the only option. She was very reluctant to make the move. Her paranoia seemed quite reasonable to me; there *was* a general plot to reorganise her life. I felt treacherous, driving her to the home, though I'd searched high and low to find the best place available. She knew there was more going on than a short recuperation.

My diary entries of that period were laden with guilt and resentment. Like me, my mother had been an intelligent and capable person. Long after my father had left, I remembered her sitting in a chair pulled up beside the heater, marking piles of school-work. Her gold-rimmed glasses gleamed as she glanced up at me with a preoccupied smile. *Off to bed, Sara? How time flies! I should have had these assignments marked by now.* I guess I'd have liked her to put the papers aside and chat a while, but at ten years old I understood that bills had to be paid and that, above all, work came first. Her example forced me to face the restricted future and the hardships my little girl could expect if I selfishly said I was going to keep her. I gave her up because my mother said she felt it would be best. So, what was she doing, reneging on me like this, just when we might finally find time to get to know each other? I didn't want a mother who pouted like a child, dribbled her food and drink, and forgot every responsibility, including me. How could she look at me with that vacant expression? How dare she forget my name!

Last Saturday, my confusion cleared. Abandoning her was wrong. I had to bring her back into my life. If we did no more than pass an hour together, I had tried. Perhaps she might know that. Now, mixing up scones and teacake, I was doubtful. Was this performance for my mother or for myself? Quite frankly I was dreading the outing. How do you control a person without rational processes to call upon? As the morning passed a knot of anxiety tightened in my stomach. Rather than force down lunch I took Molly walking, then went from room to room, reviewing my mental list. Afternoon tea, all ready; needles and wool, in case she remembered how to knit; the morning paper and television, as a last resort.

★　★　★

Martin and the boys came over at one o'clock. We dropped Adam and Bruce outside the movies and went on to the rest home where we returned the greetings of several old people sitting out in the weak sunshine. Why couldn't Mum be one of them? Frail and in need of care, they still had their faculties and their dignity. Inside, a pink-uniformed girl, about Melissa's age, unlocked the ward.

I murmured to Martin, 'Sorry to drag you here,' and he raised his eyebrows. 'I don't like hospitals,' I babbled on. 'It's worse when it's your own mother in here.'

He was seemingly unfazed by the dismal smells and depressing atmosphere.

'I guess we'll all end up like this one day,' he said. I think he meant to reassure me.

Mum had been readied for the big outing. She was sitting in her chair, the pink slippers and sagging brown stockings odd accessories to the hat and coat she always wore for best. But she'd been made tidy and presumably was well padded with whatever they used to soak up accidents.

'Hello Mum, I'm Sara,' I said firmly. Her eyes squinted as though she had trouble focusing.

'What have you done to your hair?' She sounded disapproving. 'You look like a boy.'

'It's the fashion.' I felt reassured.

'Fashion?' She stuck her feet out in front of her. 'How's this for fashion?'

'Where are your shoes, Mum?'

'Slippery soles.' The nurse intervened as though we were alone.

I rummaged at the back of the wardrobe and wiped the dust from a pair of leather dress shoes. Stubbornly I fitted them while

163

the nurse stood back, arms folded. 'We don't want any falls.' She spoke as though I was an idiot.

'There should be a handbag somewhere.' Mum never went anywhere without her capacious carryall.

'Purses are in the safe.'

'Can't you get it out?'

'Sorry. I'm not allowed the key. I'll bring the wheelchair.'

'We can walk!' I was feeling angry. These were such basic rights. The nurse gave me a nervous look and whizzed off.

'Can your mother walk?' Martin asked.

'I don't see why not. She's not a cripple.'

We helped her upright and she took several faltering steps. As far as I could tell, there was nothing wrong with her legs except lack of use. We had to wheel her as far as the front door (a hospital rule, it seemed) but from there she stumbled across to the car park, Martin and I toting her along like a shop dummy until we loaded her into the back seat and buckled up the seat belt. My fear that she might break loose and try to jump out evaporated. I could see her in the rear-vision mirror, smiling as she peered out at the scenery like any prisoner just out of gaol.

13

Martin

It was June. So far there'd been no snow but we were living a thousand metres above sea level and the frosts were biting in. In town, red-nosed students tramped about in long overcoats, boots and gloves. Neither of us was outfitted for this climate and I had to spend a fortune on clothing that we'd have no use for when we moved back to the coast. Carol had sent me a perfunctory letter from the Northern Territory, and posted a card and money to Adam, who was about to turn thirteen. She'd made it clear that for now our son was my responsibility; she'd done her bit and planned to keep travelling until her money ran out. Her attitude rather shocked me. Although I didn't like her knowing my every move, I'd never made myself unavailable to her or my son. I always took care to leave a contact address or phone number; not always conveniently, I might add. People may not change but we were certainly undergoing a role reversal now. I accepted my duty to look after Adam, supervise his homework, pay for riding lessons. When I'd suggested teaching him guitar he jumped at the offer and proved adept.

I knew I would never make a musician out of Bruce, though he tried hard enough. I asked him casually one day when I might see the next chapter of his 'novel' but he hedged and said he'd been too busy with schoolwork to write any more. It was probably a healthy sign. Thanks to Sara's gentle feedback, I'd stopped drawing comparisons between the boys. Now they got on well and I thought the age difference benefited them both. Adam looked up to his older peer and Bruce liked that, while Adam's bravado was drawing Bruce out of his shell. He'd risked a couple of rides around the paddock on a leading rein while Adam trotted ahead, showing off his novice skills. Sara told me Adam had a good seat. Whatever that was. He did look balanced and quite confident. Poor old Bruce tended to the bag of potatoes posture; perhaps to soften the inevitable fall. On the other hand, he was a whiz at maths and could sort out Adam's problems quickly. They went to the cinema together a couple of times, saving me the pain of their adolescent tastes.

Annie had offered to put on a spread for Adam's birthday. She thought we might all make a day of it together. I was glad of the suggestion. I'd had to turn down Adam's request for a less antiquated computer. My funds were in an appalling mess. Out of the blue I'd received advice from the strata managers of my unit in Newcastle that the whole block needed fireproofing to meet council regulations. My levy ran to thousands. With no current income, I couldn't see a bank advancing me another loan. So far my ideas for part-time work had fallen flat. I'd have to sell something, but what? I'd nothing of value in Armidale except the Gibson. My old faithful had travelled a good few miles with me. Parting would be the end of a long happy relationship; happier than the human kind, for sure! I could hardly bear to consider such a step. Before facing the inevitable, I went over to have a chat with Sara. She was a financial advisor, after all. I thought she might be able to suggest some other option.

We hadn't seen much of each other since the day of her mother's visit. I gathered she had put the old lady in a home years before, and had then stopped visiting when the poor old soul lost her mind. That was the picture Sara had drawn but it didn't altogether add up. It wasn't my place to comment. I didn't think Sara had had much to do with folk who stepped off the so-called normal road. I'd met my fair share of screwballs, talented freaks and losers in my nightclub days. Admittedly there was nothing pretty about an addict passed out in a doorway but sometimes I'd seen more humour and humanity in that world than in the judgmental life of the righteous. Certainly I'd nursed enough hangovers and skirted enough trouble to give the nod to the old saying, *There but for the grace of God* . . . Sara tended to present her life as perfect — at least until she opened up and I realised she'd had her losses too.

She was at the sink when I turned up. 'Here's your book back.' I put it on the table and grabbed a tea towel. She washed dishes as she did most things; efficiently.

'Did you enjoy it?'

'Entertaining in its way.' Neal Blewett's *A Cabinet Diary* wasn't the type of thing I'd go out of my way to read, but apparently she'd liked it and it had passed a few hours. 'Have you seen your mother again?'

She nodded. 'I really hate that she's locked up. She had a lovely front room when she moved there.'

'Have you questioned the change?'

'They say she's incontinent and she wanders. Well, she didn't here, did she?'

'I didn't see any sign of it.' I thought it better to be diplomatic. My impression of

168

Sara's mother was that she was dotty. She had no idea where she was or, I think, who Sara was.

'I'll bet they leave her unattended and then blame her if she has an accident.'

'You do hear about abuse in institutions. *One Flew Over the Cuckoo's Nest* type of thing.'

'I don't mean abuse.' She turned guilt-stricken eyes on me. 'I just feel bad. I turned my back on her.'

'You've made amends. Your mother seemed to enjoy her outing.' That was true enough. She'd relished her sponge cake and watched a cartoon show with keen attention. On an impulse I'd fetched my guitar and played a few of the old songs. She perked right up and said I showed promise. She'd hummed along with me to *Waltzing Matilda*.

'You have a nice way with old people,' Sara had said afterwards. I'd hoped her grateful look might lead to other things. But after we'd dropped off her mother and collected the boys she said she had bookwork to see to and that was the end of that.

She finished wiping the bench and turned to me. 'Martin. I've been meaning to thank you for the other day. You were a great support.'

I raised my eyebrows. Women have called

169

me many things but never a support!

'I thought I might take her out of care and move her into the flat, once you go.'

'I'd give that one careful thought, if I were you.' Apart from the problems I thought Sara would be letting herself in for, I felt a sudden pang. Life here was settled. Raising Adam gave my life structure and he was responding. I saw the Marshalls regularly. In their individual ways, Annie, Ben and Bruce had each made me feel I contributed somehow to their family life. I'd thought Sara might feel the same way. Her casual reference to my leaving hurt. I wasn't ready to go. Annie had said no more about Bruce, but I guessed she was only biding time while I sorted out my thoughts.

I couldn't produce any fatherly feelings for the boy. As I watched him assault his guitar or plod around the paddock on the horse, I'd think *Can he possibly be my son?* Then I'd shelve the problem. I might struggle with Adam, but at least my place in his life was clear to me.

I remembered why I'd come to consult Sara, and told her about the levy. 'I can't see any solution except to sell off the Gibson, though that might take time.'

'No work in the pipe-line yet?'

'I've drawn a blank so far.' My ideas for the

tour brochures had fallen flat.

'Could you redraw on the equity in your unit?'

'I bought when the market was inflated. There's a price slump now.'

'Savings? Shares?'

'No.'

'What about a personal loan?'

'I doubt a bank would be willing. I'm not working at present.'

'Would a friend lend you the money?'

She was full of ideas and not one applied to me. I didn't have wealthy friends nor would I ever dream of using friendship to ask financial favours. 'I'll sort it out somehow.'

'That's all I can think of. Want a coffee?'

'No thanks. Adam's waiting. I promised I'd give him a hand with an assignment. He'll be thirteen next week.'

'We must organise a treat for him.'

'We're spending the day with the Marshalls.'

I saw her conceal a look of hurt. It was true that she'd become quite involved in Adam's life. 'Why not join us? Annie's got some day trip planned.'

'No thanks.' She sounded cool. 'I'm busy, the next few weeks.'

It was my cue to leave. I gave Adam a hand with his history assignment and then settled for an early night. A sudden cloudburst rattled overhead and I lay back in bed, thinking about the Marshalls. I had no idea what to do about Bruce. He was hardly an unwanted waif. Annie and Ben were doting parents, but I couldn't see their marriage surviving if the truth came out. As for Bruce . . . A lad might be confused by having two fathers.

★   ★   ★

Ben picked us up on Adam's birthday.

'Day off?' I enquired. 'You must get tired of shift work.'

Ben hesitated. 'I've left the mine.'

'I had no idea. So what are you doing?'

'One or two interviews lined up. What about you?'

'Keeping busy.'

Whatever had happened, Ben didn't want to talk about it. His family would feel the financial pressure, unless he'd received a payout. It wasn't my business. I had my own money problems.

Adam sat squeezed between us on the front seat of the ute. For once he'd dropped the surly expression and looked happy. He was fitted out in my gift; new Nikes and jeans, and the Billabong sweatshirt Sara had bought for him. Remembering that slog of a bike ride I'd taken a few months earlier, I watched flat paddocks stretching away beneath the pallid winter sky. At home, Ben pulled up in a spurt of dust, sending hens scrambling in all directions. The old collie was methodically working on a bone, and poor old Douglas sat parked in the wheelchair in his accustomed spot on the veranda.

Ben spoke quietly in my ear. 'I'd be glad if you keep quiet about the work business. Annie's a worrier. I prefer to tell her when I'm set with another job.'

So it hadn't been a voluntary move. I nodded. It was just another little secret to add to the agenda. Bruce ran out to welcome Adam.

'Got you a cool birthday present. Can we give it to him now, Mum?'

'I suppose.' On the steps, like a '50's image of wifely welcome, Annie stood holding Joanne's hand. 'Just a second-hand thing,' she murmured to me. The boys dashed up the steps and ran into the house.

'Do you want me to check that battery for you, love?' Ben asked.

'You go ahead, Ben. I'll let you know when we're ready to leave.' She added in an aside to me, 'Ben's not coming with us today.'

'Why?' I didn't altogether trust Annie's agenda.

'He's going to keep an eye on Dad.'

'Where's Nina?'

'Having a few days' break. Dad's pretty demanding.'

'I expect she'll enjoy the rest.' I remembered the scene in the coffee shop. If she were spending the weekend alone, I'd be surprised. Douglas sat staring into space; whatever his handicaps and personality defects, I wondered at the private hell he must inhabit.

Annie filled me in on the day's plans. We were to pack a picnic and visit the bushranger display in the Uralla museum. 'It was closed when you went there with that woman.'

'You mean my friend Sara?' I had to tease her. She took no notice. 'We can drive out to Thunderbolt's hide-out cave afterwards.'

'The villain's den? Sounds right up Adam's street.'

She laughed. 'There's a bit of the robber in all of us, don't you think?'

Adam came running from the house. 'Dad! I've got my own computer, a Pentium, with heaps of games.'

I stared. 'Don't be silly, mate. That belongs to Bruce.'

'He gave it to me. He's got a new one.'

Annie intervened. 'I told you, Martin, it's second-hand. We updated Bruce's recently. The old one's just gathering dust.'

* ⋆ ⋆

I felt outclassed and, worse, suspicious. If this was the level of giving expected, where did that place me in regard to Bruce?

'Surely you could have sold it?'

'You can't give them away once they're superseded. Let Adam have it.'

'We can get the Internet, Dad.'

'We'll see.' How could I spoil Adam's obvious delight? I let him drag me off to inspect the booty, which included a CD-ROM and printer, apparently in working order. I didn't believe for a minute that Annie couldn't have sold the package. I would have paid a few hundred dollars for it myself. It was a better outfit than my own.

'Isn't it cool, Dad?'

'It runs really slowly.' Bruce was assertive in his role of benefactor. I left the pair setting up the equipment and went back to Annie.

'He's obviously over the moon.'

'You seem bothered, though.'

'Why are you doing all this for Adam?'

She fixed me with those deep blue eyes. 'We go back a long way, don't we? Bruce obviously likes you. Why shouldn't I be interested in your son?'

I suppose she was saying that, if things had gone differently, these would be our children.

'I can't reciprocate, that's all.'

'Who's counting? You think Ben and I are poor no-hopers, don't you?'

'Of course I don't.'

'New cars and designer fashion aren't our priority.' That was obviously a dig at Sara. 'We're not poverty-stricken, Martin. Ben earns good money and I've got my cleaning job. We get by.'

She was right. Privately I had filed the Marshalls just as Annie suggested. She always could see through me. Truth was, professional man though I was, my finances were much worse than theirs. I guess I'd carried a frugal childhood forward. Though Annie's upbringing wasn't generous either, she must have opted to give her children everything she'd been denied. Her attitude made me feel mean-spirited.

I waited while she packed food into picnic baskets.

'That's finished. Just the cake to ice. Grab a couple of beers and keep Ben company. I won't be long.'

'I'm not drinking, Annie. I have to give it away. I'm an alcoholic.'

There it was. My voice was calm. The words were ordinary. I'd always said I could give up drinking. In fact, I had a battle on my hands. Every day I craved whisky. If it hadn't

176

been for Adam, I'm sure I'd have weakened, but a boozer for a father was no example to set him. I didn't want alcohol around. Knowing Adam, it would only lead to experimentation. Carol must have built up a pretty unflattering picture of me. I wanted my son to respect me.

Annie tipped out the last of the chocolate icing and passed the bowl to Joanne.

'Have a can of Coke then,' was all she said. She didn't ask questions or offer advice. Such matter-of-fact acceptance really touched me. Somehow she managed to take me as I came, without the usual mission to fix or change me. That *Have a can of Coke* was about as close to a declaration of real love as I'd ever received from anyone.

'I do appreciate the effort you've gone to,' I said. 'Adam's thrilled.'

'Honestly!' She laughed and gave me a push. 'Now go! Out of my kitchen, Martin Ainsworth.'

I collected my Coke and Ben's beer, and wandered outside, feeling strangely light. If secrets were the order of the day here, at least, out in the open, they didn't seem so bad.

14

Sara

I went to the doctor's yesterday to find out my test results.

The surgery was a small room, lit by a cold fluorescent strip. A metal lamp on a flexible stem stood at the bottom of the narrow examination bed. My medical records, covered in the usual cryptic scribbles, were open centre-stage on the desk beside the phone, drug reps' pens and stationery. No family photos, no little vase of flowers. If my doctor had a personal life it wasn't on display during business hours. I could understand that. If you had to deliver unpleasant news, you'd want to bring as little as possible of your home life to work.

Helen motioned towards the second seat and came straight to the point.

'Your results are back, Sara. I'm afraid they're positive for Factor Five Leiden.'

I tried to look intelligent and curious, while something akin to panic began to grow inside me. I'd been so sure this was a wild-goose investigation. I'd never had the slightest sign of clotting problems. In fact, I'd already composed a draft letter to my daughter. I had thanked her for the information and said I was exempt from the disorder. That would mean the defect came from her father's side. I would pass on any information she might want. I also said I thought of her so very often and still hoped she would allow us a chance to meet.

Whether the agency would ever forward the letter or whether she would deign to answer it was an unknown. I'd deliberately planted the hook of her father's identity. Never had I expected this news. Helen was calmly spelling out possible complications. Venous thrombosis. Gall bladder dysfunction. Stroke. Heart attack. She sounded like a waitress at a fast-food order window.

'I've checked back through your records, Sara. I can't find any of this type of problem to date.'

She was a thorough GP; she would have done her homework well. I'd only been seeing her for the past two years and rarely needed to go to a doctor anyway.

'You're not on oral contraceptives?'

'Not for several years.' I didn't add that, since the episode with Martin, I'd been reconsidering. But so far it seemed only that — an episode.

179

'You can't take them now. They increase clotting problems. Are there strokes or coronaries in the family history?'

'I believe my father may have had a heart condition.' It was a long time ago, and all hearsay. I couldn't ask my mother now.

'Another possibility is toxaemia in pregnancy. Do you have any children? Oh, of course, it was your daughter who prompted your referral, I think?'

'She was adopted. I was barely sixteen. So she must have inherited this from me?'

'It would seem so.' A secret voice of accusation was whispering to me.

So Mother doesn't just give her baby away, she passes on a hereditary defect into the bargain?

'What's the treatment?'

'We can't cure it. What we do is monitor you for any symptoms. Drug therapy's available to discourage blood clots forming but that needs careful weighing up.'

'In what way?'

'If you had a serious car accident, for example, you'd be at greater risk of haemorrhage.'

Choose, Sara. A clot in the brain or bleeding to death?

'Medication may not be necessary. After all, you've never manifested symptoms so far.

180

You might be one of the lucky people who never do.'

Yes Sara, lucky, lucky you!

'I'll refer you to a haematologist. He'll go through the options with you.'

She wrote briskly, addressed a small white envelope and passed it to me, discreetly unsealed. A modern physician. I thanked her and left the room, my shock fading to hollow apprehension. I was emerging from a horror movie. The stalker had stepped off the screen. He was tracking me into the street, towards my car. He would go with me, biding his time to strike me down.

At home I ran another Internet search. The condition was like a lucky dip. Take your pick. Pulmonary embolism. Deep vein thrombosis. Stroke. Coumadin seemed to be the main drug of choice. Its side effects included thinning hair, fatigue, light sensitivity, and depression. There was a support group e-mail address. I sat inert, staring at the blank screen, switched off and made myself a cup of coffee.

I'd always been healthy. I ate well, took supplements, got plenty of exercise riding and walking Molly. Apart from the birth, I'd never been in hospital. If I caught a cold I was the type to soldier on. I'd never thought much about illness.

What if? whispered that demoralising voice. What if you have a stroke and find yourself in a wheelchair, unable to walk or speak? What if a clot travels to your heart? What if you take the medication and then have a car crash? What if you ever become pregnant again?

The letter I had prepared for my daughter needed redrafting now. It was in my desk drawer. As I took a fresh sheet of paper, tears started streaming down my cheeks. A terrible feeling of urgency seized me. What if she'd changed her address? What if we never did get the chance to meet and face the past? I wanted so much to explain to her. How righteous society was at that time! Young solo mothers still faced great problems, but at least now they were allowed that basic right, to know their child.

I wrote that letter, telling my daughter about the results of the test. I said that I shared her defect. We were the same. I wanted so much to meet her. Would she give me that chance? I would be available to her, wherever she now lived.

I couldn't find anything else to say. My tears had dripped onto the page. I dried them with a tissue. I was a stranger to her. Emotion might alarm her. The words hadn't smudged. I sealed up the letter, then enclosed it in a second envelope. I wrote a brief note, asking the contact agency to forward my communication to her if they knew her current address. I stressed the medical aspect of my request. It seemed more valid, somehow. I sealed up the second envelope, addressed it to the Sydney office and went straight out to post it. From there I headed over to see a client.

Of course everyone else would see me as the same old Sara. I wasn't ready to broadcast my news. Life seems endless when you're young and healthy. When you discover your body is no longer whole, it's a sorrowful moment, like watching a life-long friend turn and walk away. You think *One day, sooner, later, I'm going to die and I'll have no say at all in the moment. No vitamins, no moderation, no stress-free environment will make a whit of difference. Tomorrow or in fifty years, it's all the same. I'm not going to be here forever.*

Did my mother feel as anxious when she first recognised symptoms of her failing mind? She wasn't old. I suppose she was frightened as names and dates slipped from memory. What if other people noticed her lapses? What if they found out she'd forgotten the name of the Prime Minister? Wasn't that what they always asked you when they were suspicious? Where was that money she'd hidden? Had she given those rings to Sara or put them away somewhere? They'd disappeared. How could she make herself remember pension dates, birthdays, all that tiresome trivia people set so much store by? Write notes! That was the solution. *Put out garbage on Tuesday.* But when was Tuesday? Observe, observe! Take a peek out the window and watch the neighbours. One problem solved, a dozen in its place. *Turn off iron. Check water level in kettle. Lock doors at night. Remember to get dressed after breakfast. Remember to read notes. Remember to write notes.* Above all, cultivate a vague, pleasant expression to cover all incoming information while searching memory banks for possible response.

My poor mother! Why hadn't I understood her pain? Mental deterioration must have been slow agony for a woman who prided herself on intelligence, independence and a spotless home. Inevitably everything ran down. I remembered a particular day I called in. Perhaps I'd been sitting exams. A few weeks had elapsed since my last visit. I'd brought a teacake. Mum seemed pleased to see me and fiddled about, insisting she make the tea. I put the iced bun on a plate and carried it through to the dining table; a family piece of rich oak that she rubbed up weekly with a thick beeswax polish. As I set down the

184

plate I stared. I could have written my name in the dust on that once glowing surface. I think that was the moment when months of previous suspicions and concerns crystallised. I knew something here was very wrong. But how long had she known, and what fears had she faced alone, while her mind was still clear enough to foresee the future of a woman who could not manage as she used to?

Now her state of mind varied from visit to visit. I'd taken her out on two occasions. The first time, when I was really apprehensive and Martin kindly came with me, I didn't know what to expect. It went quite well. Mum seemed to enjoy herself and there were no dramas. I began to feel the hospital had misled me and even wondered about setting Mum up in the flat when Martin eventually vacated. The second time, I picked her up alone. We took a drive around the city and I made a point of showing her familiar places and landmarks. When we went home for afternoon tea, I found she'd wet herself and had to fit her out with a clean pad in the bulky incontinence pants she wore. She didn't want anything to eat and seemed anxious, wandering around, forlornly examining everything as though she missed the familiar surroundings of her dismal little room. *Do you want to go back to the Home?*

I suggested and for the first time all afternoon she smiled and nodded.

I was afraid the outing had unsettled her but the staff were quite unperturbed when we arrived back early. *She has her good and bad days.* Afterwards I was surprised by how tired I felt. She was constant work. Like a small child, I suppose. It wasn't possible to leave her unsupervised for five minutes. I decided to shelve the studio option and just pay a quick visit the next weekend. Melissa was booked to play at an afternoon wedding and had invited herself to dinner afterwards, which I was looking forward to.

⋆ ⋆ ⋆

Rumbles of distant thunder and a navy blue sky heralded the forecast storm as I planned Melissa's favourite meal; apricot chicken with steamed rice, followed by a Queen pudding and cream. I was scraping out the meringue topping when she was dropped off. A departing horn blast sent Molly racing to the door as Melissa walked in, lugging her cello case. She set down a bottle of riesling and peered over my shoulder.

'Leave a bit for me to lick?'

I laughed and handed her the bowl. 'How was the wedding?'

She shivered in her formal performance frock. 'Freezing! The bridal party had to do a photo marathon in some park after the ceremony, poor things. How long till dinner? Is Martin coming?'

'No.' I saw her enquiring look. 'He's just a friend, that's all.' I had considered inviting him. In his way he'd been encouraging, helping me come to decisions about my daughter and my mother. But, apart from that one time, there'd been no more physical approaches. Something odd was going on between him and Annie. I wasn't the only one pre-occupied with past issues.

Melissa just shrugged. 'I'm starving! Didn't fancy wedding leftovers. Roz thinks I've gone on to the reception.'

'Why?' I couldn't see why Melissa would need to concoct a lie.

'She expects me to stay home and wait on her hand and foot. She doesn't like being an invalid.'

'So she's had the surgery?' I suppose I could have gone through the motions, taking fruit and flowers, but I felt no warmth towards Roz. She still affected me like those intermittent thunderclaps, heralding the storm.

'A cancellation came up. They did her last week. She's home, and really grumpy.'

'Are you nurse?'

'Dogsbody! Bring this, cook that. Nothing suits. She wanted me to cancel this gig, and stay home with her. I told her we'd been booked a month ago and all she said was *Anyone can play the fucking wedding march. I'm in pain!*'

That certainly sounded like Roz. Melissa saw my amusement and conceded, 'She hates being sick.'

'Nobody enjoys it,' I said evenly. I would keep my own medical news off the agenda. Melissa was clearly lapping up the chance to be waited on. As I opened the oven door, she sniffed with pleasure.

'Apricot chicken! You're a sweetie.' She crouched down and snuggled Molly into the crook of her arm. 'God, it's nice to be home!'

'Go and put some music on. I'll be in soon.'

'Want a glass of wine?'

'Why not? Dinner isn't quite ready. Turn up the fire. I'll check the casserole, then tell me all your news.' I left her stretched out on the couch, Molly beside her, the fire glowing and music playing.

Later we were preparing to wash up when the phone rang. It was a long-distance call; a woman asking for Melissa. I passed over the mobile.

'Mara!' She sounded surprised. So the caller was Paul's wife. I discreetly left the room and began stacking plates. Melissa was only on the phone for a minute.

'That was Dad's wife.'

'What did she want?'

'Dad's missing.' She sounded concerned.

'What do you mean, missing?'

'Mara hasn't seen or heard from him since yesterday. She thought he might be here.'

'Why would Paul be here?'

'To visit me, I guess. She's really worried. She's going to contact the police.' She hesitated. 'Sara, you don't think anything's happened to him, do you?'

'Of course not. There'll be a rational explanation. Perhaps he needs time out?'

'He wouldn't just disappear without saying anything. Dad's not like that.'

She was right. It was very odd. 'Mara said she'll ring back as soon as she has any news.'

I washed and she dried. Paul was very present with us both, reminding me that we never quite leave behind the people we once loved. Melissa broke the silence.

'Sara? Don't you think it's strange, Dad just disappearing?'

'It does seem odd.' I was remembering Paul's words; *Tell Melissa I'm sorry.* Sorry for what? The words seemed ominous.

'What would happen if he doesn't come back?'

189

'I suppose the police would make enquiries and list him as a missing person.'

But Paul wasn't the kind of man to cut his ties and go somewhere incognito. It was impossible that he'd be caught up with crime or blackmail. The most likely event would be an accident, but even that made little sense. His vehicle would have been found and surely his wife would have checked the hospitals before alarming Melissa. The only other possibility was self-inflicted harm. He was an intelligent man. Surely he would see beyond his present setbacks? Even if depression had darkened his judgement, I thought he was simply too civilised to resort to the violence one would have to turn against oneself to end one's life. Wasn't this the stuff of television?

As rain squalls and gusty winds lashed the house, Melissa stood at the window, staring into the darkness.

'I don't feel like going back to the caravan. The bunk's so narrow!'

'Stay the night here.'

'I should go back. Mum's on her own.' She seemed to be considering her options. 'Sara, is it OK if I move back with you soon?'

'Your bedroom's ready when you are.'

'I think I'll have a shower. Don't fancy the amenities block at midnight.'

'Go ahead. I'll make coffee.'

The steady hiss from the shower joined the cloudburst pelting on the roof. Melissa emerged in a cloud of steam and perfumed talc, looking much more at home in jeans and my old angora sweater.

'I borrowed this. OK?'

I nodded and passed the after-dinner mints.

'Guess I'll move back home next week,' she said and I nodded, unable to repress the small moment of triumph.

15

Martin

I hardly recognised Ben when he walked Bruce up the driveway for his next music lesson. In business shirt and tie and carrying a briefcase, he looked quite the man about town. He wanted me to write him a reference for some interviews he'd lined up. I gathered the family now knew he was unemployed. It would have been a hard secret to maintain, given the nature of the job. I wondered how Annie had taken the news.

'Wouldn't your last employers be the ones to state your work skills?' I said.

Like clergy and JPs, teachers are often called on for references and it's a hard request to turn down. But in Ben's case I hardly knew the man.

'I was thinking something personal,' he suggested.

'Good bloke, pillar of the community?'

He laughed. 'That's it. Bruce did me up a CV on the computer.'

He offered a professional-looking document

from the briefcase and scanned my face for approval. It was the usual spiel. He'd had quite a few jobs by the look of things. I handed it back and he thumbed the pages as though unused to reading. 'See, the references are at the back.'

He reminded me of an eager pupil. There was a school-leaver's certificate, followed by two hand-written and poorly worded testimonials to the effect that Ben Marshall was punctual, reliable and well liked. The most recent was dated 1986.

'You could do with more,' I agreed. 'I'd get a reference from the mine. By the way, there's a gap in your work history.' The years between 1990 and 1992 had been omitted.

'You noticed? I had a bit of trouble then.'

There was a pause. 'Dad went to jail,' Bruce said flatly. I didn't know what to say. Ben's expression was closed.

'It was an accident, could've happened to anyone.'

'But the man died.'

'I know he died, son! D'you think I'll ever forget it? If that bastard I worked for hadn't put us on such a tight schedule it would never have happened.' He turned a look of dark and helpless anger on me. 'I was driving big rigs for a freight company. Hauling long-distance, Brisbane to Melbourne sort of run. Struck road works, didn't see the traffic banked up. Went into the back of a car just as the driver decided to step out.'

'He got smashed all over the road,' Bruce said with juvenile relish.

'It wasn't drink or drugs. Happened in a flash. Around that time there'd been a run of semitrailer accidents. I just happened to cop the flack.' Ben thrust the CV back into his bag. 'Funny thing, the way the past dogs you. You're right, any employer will ask questions.' He turned slowly. 'I'll get going then.'

'Hang on!' I said. The Marshalls' life hadn't struck me as easy but I'd never imagined they'd survived such a terrible experience. My own drink-driving charge had ended in no more than a reprimand and a fine. That I hadn't killed anybody was probably good luck. I could see through Ben's eyes how that nightmarish moment would have been — the body weary, the brain pushed past accurate judgement, the understanding that he'd hit the brakes too late, and all that followed.

'Come in. I'll write that reference now.'

He followed me in to the living room where I quickly opened a new computer file and started typing. When I'd printed out the sheet, Ben read it and nodded.

'Thanks, mate.'

I'd only dashed off a couple of generalised paragraphs that wouldn't count for much with a discerning employer. I couldn't write the truth; that Ben Marshall was a victim of circumstance, whose wife had chosen him out of convenience, whose lack of education condemned him to hard menial work, and whose employers had pushed him beyond his limits to become a scapegoat for society.

'Good luck with the interviews.'

His dark eyes brightened. 'Jobs with the Departments of Agriculture and Forestry. I'd really like to get into one of those areas.' He considered his square palm as though eyeing a sapling he might plant and nurture. ''Fraid I haven't got the right bits of paper.'

'Experience counts.'

'Let's hope so. I won't hold you up. Thanks again.'

★   ★   ★

I gave Bruce his lesson. He had improved slightly, though his struggle was painful to watch. His left hand seemed to find the most cramped and awkward angles possible.

'Swivel your thumb back here.' I demonstrated. 'It's locking up the whole hand.'

He copied me but within five minutes reverted to habit. I reminded him and he

195

slapped the side of his head.

'Idiot! Reckon I'll nail my thumb in place.'

'Habits are hard to break.' Well, I knew all about that. 'Ease up a bit, Bruce.'

The boys wandered outside after the lesson. I made myself a coffee and sat down with the newspaper by the window. The weak sunshine offered little warmth but I thought of the power bill and resisted turning on the heater. I was starting to think like Scrooge. I scanned the local news and the Classifieds, passing over an advertisement for a permanent teaching position at a local secondary school. Jobs in the area were limited. Ben would have to compete with applicants who had degrees or TAFE courses. He was the modern-day equivalent of Thomas Hardy's Jude; a decent man unable to lift himself above labouring because of the circumstances of his birth. Stone masonry was a dirty job, like a miner's. Funny how little had really changed in a hundred years. This country was supposed to be egalitarian. Schooling was said to be free, yet tertiary education fees had climbed steeply and private schools were the domain of professional parents' children. I knew Annie was determined to set her children on a road with options, but Ben was faltering. How could he possibly maintain the standards she'd set?

I glanced at the vehicles for sale and suddenly realised I'd found the solution to my financial problems. So simple! My car was garaged in Newcastle, awaiting my return. I'd simply forgotten about it. Here I was managing very well with public transport, a bicycle or Shank's pony. A quick trip would set the sale in motion. At the same time I could check on the unit and pick up a few items from storage. I wouldn't take Adam out of school. Sara would give him dinner and keep an eye on him. I'd only be away one night.

Vastly relieved, I went down by train a few days later and saw to the business immediately. My tenant allowed me free access to the unit, and the first dealer who came to inspect the car bought it on the spot. Holding my cheque for $4000, I signed the change of ownership papers and heard him drive away. The vehicle was worth more, but he'd played up the spot of rust and the noisy exhaust. I wasn't in a position to barter.

Inspecting the unit was like observing one's ex-wife with a new partner. I didn't much like the leopard-print bedcover or airbrush art, though the place was clean and tidy. Seiko came running, sleekly fat. My little cat was the only thing I missed. I longed to scoop her up and take her with me, along with the few books and CDs I'd packed. Peter came home around five o'clock. I listened, politely bored, to long-winded tales about staffing levels, timetables and the curriculum. No doubt I'd once filled many social hours with similar monologues. We went out for a bistro meal, where Peter probed my plans for returning to the school. My former life here felt unreal and I could only give vague answers, though I knew he had his own career to consider. A little put out by my evasions, he switched on TV and we watched a current affairs programme, Seiko curled up on my knee. I turned in early. Lying on the uncomfortable spare bed, I felt sorry for past guests who'd been too polite to tell me the slatted base felt like the rack. Footsteps clattered in the upstairs unit. Finally I fell asleep.

When we said goodbye, Peter asked again when I was planning to return. Spring, I suggested. That would be the official end of my leave but I had the feeling I was mouthing words. I was to catch the train from Broadmeadow just before midday. With hours to fill, I took a long walk, noting changes even in the short time I'd been away. The BHP was due to close. Newcastle was having a make-over, its industrial image giving way to tourism and inner city apartment blocks. High-rise hotels were claiming the best views in the East End. At least the route to Nobbys beach hadn't altered much. Stacked terrace houses lined the tranquil old streets. The sea front was still dramatic, with its pounding breakers and surfers riding the waves. On the horizon, a dozen container ships waited for permission to enter harbour.

At this time of the morning there weren't many people around — a jogger, a sedate old couple and their portly Labrador. I walked out towards the lighthouse. The massive rocks of the sea wall were said to have originated in America; thrown up in the great California earthquake and transported as ballast in sailing ships. One could only imagine the suffering behind the present postcard prettiness. Shackled convicts must have stared in despair at their watery prison before bending their backs to build this breakwater.

When the town clock chimed eleven, I turned, standing for a moment to face the hilly cityscape, crowned by the Anglican cathedral and the asterisks of dark Norfolk pines. I felt I was saying goodbye to an old camping ground. Three months before, I'd travelled north with the burden of my court appearance and my poor relationship with Adam. This time the journey was more enjoyable. My finances were back on track. I looked forward to getting home to Adam and

Sara. Money in my wallet made a big difference to my feelings. I could pay the bills with cash to spare. In return for all of Sara's help with Adam, I could treat her to a decent restaurant.

★ ★ ★

At Armidale station, I was welcomed by a bitter winter wind and hurried into a taxi. My flat was in darkness. I went over to Sara's and Melissa came to the door. I followed her in to the living room, where Adam was sprawled on the floor, watching a variety show on TV.

'Hi Dad!' He kept his eyes on the screen, where some idiot was chewing up glass tumblers.

'Sara's at a meeting,' Melissa said.

'Thanks for minding Adam. I had to make an urgent trip.'

'No problem. Sara told me. Anyway, I've moved back now, it wasn't any trouble.'

Her manner was withdrawn and I hoped Adam hadn't been misbehaving.

'Let's go,' I suggested to him. 'Better give Melissa some peace.'

But he was engrossed. 'Cop this, Dad!' The glass-eater had changed his diet to handfuls of nails.

Melissa intervened. 'Let him finish the show. Coffee?'

The phone rang. She ran to answer it and came back dejected.

'It was for Sara.'

It was obvious that she was waiting for a call. Perhaps she had boyfriend issues. She seemed on the verge of tears and I asked her what was wrong.

'My father's disappeared. I was hoping that might be news.'

She told me he'd been missing for a week and the police had been informed.

'I should go down to Newcastle.' She sounded reluctant. 'Mara, my other step-mother lives there.'

'Get on well?'

'Not really. She's OK. She and Dad argued a fair bit, but that's the way with relationships.'

'You sound jaded!' Like most little girls she'd probably dreamed of white weddings and happy-ever-after. Her father's three marriages must have disrupted her entire growing years.

'Why wouldn't I be?'

'No room for romance?'

'Aren't you divorced?'

'*Touché!* I'm still hoping.'

'Are you? Would you get married again?'

Romance was one thing, alimony another. 'I'm no good with hypothetical questions. What time is Sara due back?'

'Not late. Do you like her?'

'Of course I do.'

'I mean, do you *like* her?'

I turned the question away. 'I don't think she likes *me* particularly.'

'Oh, she does. But she keeps bad news to herself.'

'What news is that?'

'Did she tell you she has a blood disease?'

I felt uncomfortable. 'She mentioned tests to me. Nothing else. I don't think we should be talking about Sara.'

'No.' She began to cry like a child. 'Martin, I think my father's dead.'

'People sometimes go away for a time.'

'He wasn't happy. They had awful rows. He lost his job.'

'And you think he's killed himself?'

She nodded, sobbing now. All I could do was pat her shoulder and try to reassure her. In fact, I had nothing useful to say and was relieved when Sara walked in and assessed the situation.

'Melissa? Have you heard news?'

Clearly expecting the worst, she looked relieved when Melissa shook her head.

'Nothing.' She was trying to pull herself

together. 'Sara, what if we never find out what happened?'

'We will, darling.'

I felt useless. They needed their privacy. It was time to go. Even Adam got the message and peeled himself off the rug as the show ended with a stomach-turning regurgitation of lethal objects. Sara was hugging Melissa.

'We'll be off. I hope you get news soon.' I knew Sara must be worried. After all, she'd lived with the man for a number of years, even if she wasn't one to share her problems much. We were birds of a feather in that regard and I recognised that mask as she waved goodnight. 'In fact, I'd like to take you out to dinner. Just a thank you for everything.' She hesitated and I thought she was about to knock me back.

But she smiled. 'That would be very nice,' she said.

16

Sara

Three months ago I was happy. I wasn't questioning life — my own or anyone else's. If at times I was lonely, I only had to remind myself that marriage wasn't all roses. Business was going well. My finances had really picked up. I was healthy, relatively young and fit. I didn't want a man to lean on. For that overseas trip I planned, I could travel with a group if I wanted company.

Years ago I faced the fact that even our closest connections were in the end temporary. Melissa had left home; my own mother had forgotten me. For a while, the diary I turned to after Paul left was filled with blame, analysis, and self-reproach. In time I set it aside and decided to move on. I put away all reminders of my life with Paul, drew up a five-year plan and took steps to set up as an independent financial adviser. Hard as it was, I accepted that Melissa's place was with her father. She wasn't the first child I'd lost. I put Roz and her erratic ways out of my mind.

Molly turned up about that time. I suspect she'd fallen from the back of a ute as she was limping but otherwise in good condition. My dog and I became instant best friends. My life was sorted, until my tenant and his son moved in and I was landed with another needy child. Oh, Martin didn't impose. I liked Adam and could see he felt abandoned. Children deserve security. I couldn't imagine how his mother simply left like that, or why the paternity issue mattered so much to Martin.

Of course that brought up the issue of Shannon. I'd believed that giving her up for adoption had been the best decision. Everyone had said so. But she must have blamed me; thought I was selfish and unloving. Why else had she declined to meet me? I was still waiting to hear whether she'd changed her mind. Every time I collected my mail, my heart would pound like a girl with a teenage crush. Another issue I had to face was the blood disorder. In bleak moments I saw myself stricken with paralysis, like one of those poor women at the nursing home. It was Martin who influenced me to go back and see Mum. Before I spoke to him, I was reconciled to her state, knowing she was cared for. Now I had to face the afflictions of those old people removed from normal life. I had to deal with my mother's condition, which was unpredictable and time-consuming.

Damn Martin! That impulsive evening was a mistake. What if I'd fallen pregnant? No doubt he thought I'd be well organised in that regard. In fact I hadn't had sex for years. There were a couple of fellows, after Paul, but I soon saw the futility of what I was doing and decided to keep off my back until I met someone I'd consider as a long-term partner. Who might that be? Certainly not an unemployed, broke, temporary tenant with a drinking problem and a difficult son. Martin would be gone in a few months anyway. We'd never been out on what you could call a date. What had we shared? A tense meal in his flat and a couple of outings with Annie Marshall, an odd woman I thought he had past issues with.

Martin could be charming, funny and understanding. We hit it off in bed. Well, there was nothing like fasting to make you enjoy a good meal. But I'd made sure there was no repeat performance. Stepped back. And then he asked me out to dinner and I heard myself accept.

★   ★   ★

My black Cue suit was too formal and the Perri Cutten ensemble wasn't warm enough for a July night. Melissa came in as I was searching my wardrobe.

'Tell me what to wear.' I offered one hanger after another. Everything looked wrong. I shook my head as she held up a red off-the-shoulder evening dress that I hadn't worn since Paul left.

'Why not? It's sexy.'

'I don't want to look sexy.'

It was good to hear her laugh. The worry over Paul still hung over us both. She left me re-hanging half a dozen outfits. In the end I settled on the Perri Cutten jacket and pants with arctic-thick layers underneath. I put on silver sandals and did my nails and make-up carefully before pouring a quick pre-dinner riesling. Martin was due at seven.

'Have I overdone it?' I asked Melissa.

'I see you went for sexy.'

'Dressy,' I corrected her. 'Have a glass of wine with me?'

When Martin turned up he did a double take. 'You look stunning.'

He'd dressed too, in a rather nice sports jacket and well-cut pants, though his grey tie was a peculiar choice with the brown shirt.

'Where are you two going?' Melissa asked.

'Archies on the Park. Know it?'

'They won a Tourism Council Award for Excellence just recently.' I felt flattered by his choice.

'Have a good time. I'll look in on Adam.'
Melissa settled by the fire to watch a video,
Molly curled up at her feet.

Martin laid a discreet arm around my
shoulder. 'Shall we go?'

The restaurant was a few kilometres out of
town, on the Uralla road. As I drove, Martin
chatted about his trip to Newcastle. He'd sold
a car (unbelievably he'd forgotten he owned
one) and said he'd solved his financial crisis.

'So dinner won't send you bankrupt then!'

'Not this week, anyway.'

'I've been starving myself all day. I intend
to do this meal full justice.'

'Spoken like an epicure.'

'A what?'

'A follower of Epicurus. The Greek
philosopher. He lived around 300 BC and
advocated philosophical conversation, poetry,
literature, dance and good food. And human
affection; he promoted that.'

Martin was fond of delivering little lessons.
I interrupted him to swing right and follow
the long driveway towards the parking area
of the restaurant. We hurried through the
freezing air towards welcoming lights, where
logs burned behind the glass of a circular
wood heater and a black grand piano offset
the white linen and red candles in the dining
room.

'Your Epicurus would approve,' I murmured as we were shown to a table.

The rituals of dining opened with the flick of a white napkin, the flash of light in a crystal glass and the menu presented with the solemnity of an Olympic award. How long was it since I'd been out to dinner with a man? Martin glanced at the wine list, then handed it to me.

'Choose what you like, Sara. I'll stick to mineral water.'

Apparently he was dealing with his problem. 'Mineral water will do me fine,' I offered, and he smiled at me.

'I know you enjoy a drink. Don't take my situation on board. You choose, I'm just slipping out to the Men's for a moment.'

I watched him walk across the room. He was trying hard, with alcohol, with Adam. I knew how difficult it was to face one's issues, much less resolve to mend them. I warmed towards him as I scanned the wine list.

I'd been over the selection several times and settled on a bottle of Drayton's chardonnay by the time he returned. He seemed distracted as he sat down.

'Ready to order?'

I stared. 'What about you? You haven't looked at the menu yet.'

Was he one of those men who ordered

steak and chips, regardless of the chef's imagination? He picked up the folder and vaguely scanned the printed sheets.

'Are you feeling all right?' He'd been gone for several minutes. Maybe he had a stomach bug.

'Annie's here.'

'Annie Marshall?' I wouldn't have thought she and her husband could afford to eat out at *Archies* but good luck to them! Perhaps they'd had a windfall. I was sure of one thing. I didn't want to spend the evening in their company.

'Perhaps we can sit with them for coffee afterwards?'

Martin shook his head. 'I mean, Annie's waitressing. I ran into her in the foyer.'

So that was where he'd been. It was thoroughly annoying. Wherever Martin and I chose to go, there was Annie!

'So what? It's not her business who you take out to dinner.' I knew how abrupt I must sound, but I was pushing for an answer. Martin said nothing.

'I mean, there's nothing between you, after all.'

'That's not strictly true, Sara.'

I couldn't explain how disappointed I was in him and in myself for being taken in. 'In that case, I think we should cancel tonight.' I

210

pushed back my chair but he grabbed my hand.

'Sit down! It's nothing like that. It's about Bruce.'

'Bruce? Their son?'

'That picnic at the Metz Gorge. Annie told me Bruce is mine. I mean, I'm his father. I had absolutely no idea. I'm still shattered.'

He sounded so bewildered that I sat down again. The wine waiter, who had been hovering, gingerly approached with bottle and ice bucket. As he walked away I leaned towards Martin. We were talking about confidential matters and I spoke quietly. 'Even so, why does she behave as though she owns you?'

'Annie's like that. Always was. She's single-minded. I'm part of her past and she wants to hold on.'

'We all have pasts, Martin.' Good heavens, I knew that. Of course it hurt, knowing a partner had moved on.

'But can't you see how Bruce complicates things? I can't just forget about it.'

'No.' I certainly hadn't forgotten Shannon. 'But are you sure what Annie says is true?' I wouldn't have put it past her to concoct any story.

He nodded. 'I just feel it is. The dates tally. It's an awful mess. She wants something from me.'

'She's left it rather late.' Bruce was well into his teens.

'I do feel responsible.'

'Yes. I can understand.'

We sat staring at our menus, my pleasure in the evening gone.

'I didn't mean to spring this on you, Sara.' He reached over and gently took my hand. 'I'm sorry.'

'You could have told me before.' After all, I'd told him about the adoption, and my mother.

'We tend to broadcast the good news, not the bad.'

'True.' His life was hardly an example of glad tidings — the ex-wife, the debts, the alcohol, the unhappy son. Mine wasn't much better. I lay awake at night, worrying about my mother, my health, and Shannon.

'Why the wry look?'

'What a pair! You've turned up a son, I'm searching for a daughter.'

Our conversation came to an abrupt halt as Annie loomed over us, pad and pencil poised. She spoke abruptly. 'Ready to order?'

'You first, Sara.' He was clearly uncomfortable.

'The seafood bisque entrée, I think. And the Parmesan barramundi. I assume it's fresh?' Armidale was inland and I preferred to know the use-by date of fish.

Annie gave me a sour nod. 'Vegetables?'

'Yes. And no crayfish in the entrée, please. I'm allergic.'

She looked as though she'd be delighted to see me in anaphylactic shock.

'Dessert?'

'I think I'll defer. I can always order later.' She addressed Martin. 'Yes?'

'Soup of the day, thanks. What is it?'

'Pumpkin. Main?'

'Scotch fillet.'

'Rare, medium, well-done?'

'Medium, thanks.'

'Vegetables? Salad?'

'Yes. Either. I don't care.'

I was relieved when Annie walked away.

'Not the warmest of exchanges, was it?' I mimicked her tone. 'Vegetables?'

'It's an awkward situation, Sara.'

'Don't make excuses for her. She was rude to me. If she doesn't want to serve at table, why do it?'

'Ben's out of work. We were talking about it outside. He's been knocked back on several jobs. They need the money.'

Of course Annie would be watching every mouthful we ate, comparing our bill to the cost of groceries to feed her family. She would know the price of my outfit would pay their rent or mortgage for a month.

'Will she ever let you go? She seems obsessed.'

I held in my anger. I had never behaved like that. If I had to suffer I did so quietly. Annie was blatant and Martin couldn't see it. I didn't for a moment believe Annie's interest in him was only because of Bruce, even if her story was true. Martin smiled wanly.

'Sara, I asked you out because I wanted to spend an evening with you. Can't we just forget her?'

'It's rather difficult, when she's shooting poisonous looks my way.' But I sipped my wine and smiled at him. 'Sorry, Martin. This is a lovely setting. You're right, let's enjoy it.'

★ ★ ★

And that's what we tried to do. The food was excellent. The pianist played selections from *Les Misérables* and *Phantom of the Opera*. I mentioned they were my favourite musicals and Martin gave a polite smile. Annie came and went, slapping down plates and removing the used dishes. Martin didn't mention Bruce again. Our conversation laboured on. When I'd slowed down on the Chardonnay, knowing I had to drive, he drained his mineral water and filled his empty glass with wine.

214

'Pity to waste this.' He downed it at a gulp. 'I thought you were on the wagon?'

'Yes. With an occasional lapse. I'll start again tomorrow.'

It was none of my business. It wasn't a night for good behaviour. After that unfriendly opening, I treated Annie as she had me. Martin finished the wine and loudly ordered another bottle. All we could do, as he said, was to start again tomorrow.

★　★　★

Things were little better at home. Melissa was in bed. I peeped round her half-open door and Molly thumped her tail but made no move to join us. Martin and I drank our coffee by the fire. He was rather quiet, and I filled the silence speculating about the mysterious situation with Paul.

'He's just not the type to walk away from his responsibilities.'

'Perhaps we don't know what anyone's capable of. I must say I'm at a loss, wondering what I ought to do about Bruce.'

There we were, back to the Marshalls. 'Has Annie asked you for money for his education?'

'No. Just suggested I should take an interest in him.'

'You really think that's all she expects?'

He sounded exasperated. 'You're a woman. You tell me what she wants!'

I didn't reply. Annie wanted Martin! If he didn't know that, I wasn't about to enlighten him.

I moved closer and pressed his arm. 'Thanks for a lovely evening.'

But his mind seemed far away. He reached for the travel brochures lying on the coffee table. I'd brought them home just after the news of the thrombophilia. The shock of that news had passed. I'd incorporated my defect, as I suppose most people adapt to a health crisis.

'Planning a trip, Sara?'

'Not immediately. Perhaps I'll celebrate the Millenium next year. I'd love to tour Europe and America, wouldn't you?'

'I've always fancied the East.' He riffled past photos of Trafalgar Square and the Eiffel Tower.

'A friend went to Indonesia recently. He wasn't impressed. People hawking and spitting and stray dogs fouling everywhere.'

'Unless you go Club Med I guess that's the reality.' He stood up. 'I'll make tracks. Thanks for your company.'

'It's not late. I could make more coffee.'

But he gave one of those wistful,

216

preoccupied smiles. I walked with him to the door and he left me there, dropping a light kiss on my cheek. I watched him go, stepping in his tentative way as though he wasn't quite grounded.

When I heard his front door close, I wandered back to the living room. The brochures with their bright cosmopolitan scenes and cosy couples lay open on the table. Unusually, I felt lonely. There was nothing worth watching on TV. I sat staring at a weather grid as though it held some important message for me, until I switched off, summoned Molly and we took ourselves to bed.

17

Martin

Bruce and I battled on with the lessons. By now he could fumble his way through *Ode to Joy* and *Banks of the Ohio*. He lacked natural rhythm and had to count out every beat but I supposed we were making progress. As he was waiting for Ben to pick him up, he pulled several papers from his music case and handed them to me.

'The next chapter of my novel,' he muttered, adding, 'and as well there's an invite to Mum's birthday.'

'When is that?'

'July 22nd. One week before mine. Hope you like the chapter. It's not about anyone you know.'

'Of course not.' I felt curious to read the pages straightaway; they would soon enlighten me on where young Bruce's life was at.

Ben was parked at the gate. I walked down with Bruce to ask whether he'd had any joy with the job-hunting. He was still waiting to hear, he said; we both knew what that meant.

It was while we were chatting that Melissa came running from the house, calling and waving.

'Dad's back!' She was overjoyed. 'He just phoned. He came home last night.'

'So where was he?'

'He said he had to be alone to think about his life.'

'I see.' It seemed to me that Paul must be a very selfish man to put his family through such stress while he did his private thinking.

'Isn't it wonderful?' Melissa was radiant. 'I was so worried! I must ring Sara and tell her now. I just thought you'd like to know.'

'What was that about?' From the driver's seat Ben looked after her.

'Her father disappeared. The police had him listed as a missing person. Apparently he's decided home's the better option to starting out with a brand-new identity.'

'Interesting thought but,' Ben said. 'Choosing who you'll be. I've read of people doing that. I don't know how they get away with it.'

'Fake name, fake background, dye your hair or grow a beard.'

'You'd always feel like you were on the run.'

'Maybe. Australia's a big country. Plenty of places to hide.'

'Hop in, son,' said Ben. 'Did you give Martin your mother's invitation?'

I nodded. 'I'll try and make it. A few other things on around that date.' I wasn't sure I was ready to spend a day with Annie, though it might give us a chance to discuss Bruce.

Bruce climbed up beside his father. 'Thanks, Martin. Great lesson.'

I returned his smile. Poor kid, caught in the middle of such conflict. Back in the flat I settled to read his writing.

CHAPTER TWO

'Pass that screwdriver, son,' said Tony's dad, holding out his grimy hand as he lay on the ground, examining the running-board of the 1930 Chevrolet Tourer which was his pride and joy. His hobby was vintage cars, but he couldn't afford the kind Blake's father drove. They were classy vehicles without a spot of rust; their chrome parts twinkling in the sunshine and their paintwork shining like mirrors. He had three already, a Pontiac, a La Salle sedan and a V8 Roadster, which even Tony, who wasn't much of a car fanatic, thought was cool.

'What are you doing, Dad?' Tony asked, hoping he wouldn't have to be out in the hot sun much longer. His father was tapping along the join with the handle of the screwdriver.

'Looking for weak spots. You can't get a decent price for a car if it's falling to bits.'

'But you said you want to take it on the Easter Rally! Surely you don't plan to sell it now!'

Mr Henshaw gave a heavy sigh and wiped the sweat from his forehead. 'I don't have any choice, son. Wilson's approached me privately and he's got his mind set on this car. You know we need the money.'

★　★　★

Oh no! Not Blake Wilson's father! How greedy could you get? He had three vintage cars but that wasn't enough. Tony had met him a few times. Mr Wilson was a history teacher himself at another school and got on well with teachers generally. He didn't seem to have a wife these days. Maybe she had died. A few times he'd come to talk to Tony and his mother at school prizegivings. He seemed to get on well with the ladies too. 'How did you come by such a clever son, Mrs Henshaw? I suppose he gets his brains from you?' With his grey hair and scholarly stoop he seemed a gentleman and sometimes Tony wondered why his mother hadn't married a man like Mr Wilson, who could pay her compliments and talk about Chaucer and poetry and stuff she liked. He could play an old-fashioned lute too.

But it wasn't fair that he could just take Mr Henshaw's car! What would Dad do now, without the everlasting repairs and restoration that he loved?

'Dad, I don't think you should sell the car,' Tony insisted.

'Why not?'

'Because you love it!' burst out Tony. 'It's just not fair!'

'Better talk to your mother about that. You know I'm out of work. We have to pay the bills. That's that.' Stubbornly he moved round the other side and began to tap the second running board.

Tony went inside the house, which was old and tumbledown. His mother was cooking at the stove and there was a nice appetising aroma floating around the kitchen. It made his mouth water in anticipation. She was a pretty good cook.

'What are you baking, Mum?' asked Tony, sniffing the air.

'Your favourite apple pie.' She gave him a big smile. She was always doing things for the family.

'Mum, can't you stop Dad from selling the Tourer?'

Mrs Henshaw didn't answer. Instead she opened the oven door and poked at something with a fork. When she straightened up her face looked rather red.

'You don't understand, Tony,' she said. 'You just don't understand.'

'Understand what?' He felt annoyed. He hated being talked down to like the little kids.

'What life costs.'

'What do you mean?' He was puzzled. You didn't go to some shop or Internet site and order life and pay by credit card. Life was free!

'The cost of living.' She sounded irritable. 'Let me get on with my work now.'

★　★　★

Mr Henshaw walked in to the kitchen just then and helped himself to a can of cold beer.

'Another one!' his wife said accusingly and her husband slammed the tin down on the kitchen table loudly.

'It's hot! Do you begrudge me a drink now?'

'You've already had two. Try cold water. It's free.'

'Sometimes I wonder why you married me! I've always done my best, you know that, and all you do is nag and complain.'

Tony's father stormed out and Tony went off to his room and lay on his bed. Money. He was sick of the subject. Absolutely fed up to the teeth with hearing about it. His parents talked about it all the time. Most of their fights were because there wasn't enough, or they had to pay some bill, or the kids needed stuff. There were a lot of fights these days because Tony's mother had had to get another job doing people's ironing so she was always tired and Mr Henshaw was feeling pretty bad, not having a job of his own. No wonder some people became robbers. It used to be a fairly normal thing to do. Their district used to have a famous bushranger who rode about on horseback stopping travellers and hoisting their valuables. Tony, who was a fine horseman with a good seat, imagined himself hiding out in the rocky outcrop just past the town, waiting to ambush the next coach and get his hands on heaps of jewels and money. What a surprise for his parents! It would be a lot more exciting than finishing that boring novel on economic rationalisation in Wollongong that was a set text for the scholarship exam. But then Tony felt glum. His idea was only a fantasy. There was nothing he could do to help. His mum and dad were both miserable. They were different types of people, somehow. Yes, his mother ought to have married someone like Mr Wilson, who was actually a really nice man (apart from wanting Mr Henshaw's vintage car).

* * *

I couldn't help it; I'd laughed aloud a couple of times as I skimmed the pages. No wonder Bruce had gone to such pains to stress that the work was 'fiction'. Obviously Mr. Wilson with his lute and his liking for Chaucer was none other than myself. Grey hair and scholarly stoop indeed! The young are unkindly observant of tendencies one has not yet acknowledged. At least there were no morbid references. Mr. Wilson was apparently an acceptable alternative to death in resolving Bruce's conflicts. Was he so aware of his mismatched parents? I knew from bitter experience how a growing child could view a parent with a coldly analytical eye. But as I fastened his pages with a paperclip, I thought ruefully that he'd found a poor confidant in me.

★   ★   ★

Annie's brief note had proposed an outing to Hillgrove. It would be a weekday, when the children would all be at school, so I guessed Ben and I would make up a threesome with her. Perhaps for one day of the year she felt entitled to drop the maternal role and be with adults. I couldn't imagine what had prompted the choice of Hillgrove. As far as I knew, it was an almost derelict settlement apart from the antimony mine. However, as the day approached I found myself eager to spend a day with Annie. We were old friends; we'd shared a youthful passion and Bruce linked us now. Since the night of that very awkward dinner, I found myself thinking of her often. She'd made no effort to be pleasant to Sara but, alone with me in the foyer, she'd been matter-of-fact, taking it as natural that she'd gather up the reins of earning so that her family wouldn't suffer. I thought her both brave and stoical, and just wished I had contacts to secure Ben a post somewhere.

My interest in Sara was cooling. She was attractive, smart, and kind to Adam. Bed had been pleasurable for us both. I knew the small differences that kept cropping up between us shouldn't matter. What if our tastes in books and music differed, or she set more store than I on dressing for an occasion? Must partners be carbon copies of each other? So what if she preferred the sophistication of Europe and I was drawn to Asia? It was unlikely we'd ever spend much time in either location. We eat, we sleep, we earn our keep. Although my job at the school was open, I'd wondered whether I would return at the end of my leave. The prospect of starting a new life had included Sara. Somehow in that unformulated equation, I'd hoped our dinner would be the first step in the right direction.

Without Annie, perhaps it could have been. As it was, the night at the restaurant was a disaster. Annie was abrupt, while Sara's manner, I thought, was straight from the Royals' book of protocol. Cold and aloof.

Social inequalities are never easy to watch in operation and one's heart is drawn towards the underdog — in this case my first love, whom I'd treated badly and deserted like any villain in a Victorian novel. Watching Annie go about her menial tasks, I was distanced more and more from Sara. At home, we talked a while and she indicated I could stay, but my heart wouldn't allow it. I kept thinking of poor Annie.

I cycled out early on the morning of Annie's birthday. In the carrier I had a paperback and a small posy from the florist. Armidale was short on garden blooms at that time of year. Unaffected by the pallid sunshine, horses and sheep stood bundled in their winter overcoats. A sharp wind sliced through my trouser legs and tattered the foliage of hedge breaks, where cottages huddled deep in shadow. The Marshalls' place seemed quiet. The children would be at school, and the dog and cats perhaps curled up by the fire. The ute wasn't there, nor the vintage car Ben had been restoring. At once Bruce's novel flashed into my mind.

At the door, I handed Annie her gifts and lightly kissed her cheek.

'Happy birthday.'

She tore the brown wrapper from the book. 'The new Peter Carey! And these lovely jonquils and irises . . . ' She pressed them against her face.

'The wind knocked them around a bit.'

'They're beautiful. I'll find a vase.' In the kitchen she arranged the flowers. 'Do you like this? Ben made it for me.' She showed me a wooden spice rack, stacked with glass bottles.

I nodded. 'Where is Ben?'

'Didn't I say? He's been called in to a second interview with the Council. No warning, naturally. Someone phoned late yesterday. They've whittled the applications back to three, so he stands a chance.'

'That's good. So our excursion's off?'

In my opinion it wasn't picnic weather but Annie disagreed. 'The food's ready and so am I!'

'You don't think a chat by the fire's more appealing?'

She laughed. 'City living's turned you soft, Martin. It's a perfect day. This is Armidale, remember?'

She was always impetuous, determined; traits my vacillating temperament deserved. She looked happy when I backed down. 'You win. Shall we go?'

I hadn't seen any sign of her father. As she locked up, I asked where he was.

'He's back with Mum. I can't say I'm sorry.'

'Nina enjoyed her holiday?'

'She's positively glowing. Dad's very difficult. I guess one does one's duty.'

And perhaps a little more. In any case, Nina was happy.

★   ★   ★

Annie's old Chrysler had rips in the upholstery, a windscreen wiper hanging from a piece of wire and a cracked windshield. The muffler had gone and I was relieved when she wound up her window. She seemed oblivious to it all.

'What fun! It's like old times.'

I braced myself as she slammed on the foot brake to avoid scavenging crows. It was true that we used to head off on spontaneous trips, parking on side roads to make love. As we headed out to Hillgrove, I sank into the serenity of the pale sky and ferny crannies with their glimpses of bubbling streams. Memories filled my mind until it seemed Annie and I had been on some endless journey side by side forever. We'd set out as opinionated students, full of certainties and ambition. My head was full of dreams. I suppose Annie's was too but I never asked. I was made arrogant by sexual conquest and mental stimulation yet, when reality stepped up and tapped my shoulder, I made a run for it. Had some unconscious prompt warned me off? I was quick to judge Melissa's father for his bolt; they say the actions that you dislike in others reflect your own. In any case, Annie couldn't run. She carried the responsibility for us both.

'I'm surprised you don't hate me.' I hardly realised that I'd spoken. She just reached out a hand and caressed my thigh. For minutes after she withdrew, I felt her touch, suggestive through the fabric of my trousers.

'You shouldn't have kept Bruce a secret from me all these years.'

'I didn't want you like that,' was all she said.

'Like what?'

'Duty. Doing the decent thing.'

'You accepted Ben on those terms.'

'I don't love Ben.'

I didn't know how to reply. She'd used the present tense. Could a woman maintain such pretence indefinitely?

Seemingly calm, she changed the subject. 'Let's give Hillgrove a miss. There's nothing there. Ben wanted to show you the mine and old equipment in the museum.'

I didn't care where she took me. As she swung right onto the road leading to the Metz Gorge, the exhaust rumbling, I stared passively as wary cattle and donkeys backed from fences as we passed. She parked in that same spot where we'd all gone on that other picnic. Ahead loomed the awful gulf of the gorge but here the trees formed a picturesque glade. She cut the engine and leaned back, stretching. We sat for a minute.

'Hungry, Martin?'

'So-so.'

'Let's just walk for a while.'

She gathered the picnic blanket and wicker basket. I followed her towards the trees, knowing where she was headed. There, in that same empty place, seen only by whatever birds perched hidden in the branches of old gums, I stood and waited as she set down the basket and spread the rug.

'Here we are,' she said, her blue eyes challenging mine.

'Here we are.' I yielded, acknowledging why she'd brought us to this exact spot. Annie lifted her arms and slowly fanned out her long hair. She took off her bulky cardigan and shabby boots, then opened her long dress, showing me her full veined breasts, her waist and swelling hips, her strong thighs and shapely calves. I took her in my arms and gently pressed her down onto the blanket. Compulsively my hands roamed her familiar body. She kissed me, long and deep. And after we'd made love, drained and mindless, I nestled my face into the warm cleft between her breasts.

18

Sara

Although Melissa had moved back home with me, Roz made regular claims on her time. Clearly her mother wasn't the imagined figure she'd longed for, but a needy person with expectations of her daughter. I was making similar adjustments towards my own mother. We'd tried a few more outings and I understood now that the nurses weren't callous or indifferent. There could be no lasting awakenings. Mum's powers of recall were random flickers of a burned-down candle. She had forgotten me, forgotten her whole life. Fearful of the outside world, she would never be capable of living there again. Moving her into the flat was a fantasy. I think Melissa now felt something similar about Roz. The regular calls on her time and money were wearing thin. A new man was apparently on the scene and Melissa wasn't impressed. *He has no teeth*, she'd reported. Somehow that summed things up.

We had just sat down to a breakfast of

bacon and eggs when the phone rang. We eyed each other, then our plates.

'Leave it,' I suggested. 'They can use the answerphone.'

Melissa checked the message on her way through to the shower. 'Someone for you. A Kelly Anderson,' she called, closing the bathroom door. Melissa liked long showers. As soon as I heard the drumming of water, I played back the message. I'd never heard of Kelly Anderson. Why was I so sure she was my daughter? For weeks I'd waited and waited, until the silence convinced me I should never have let Martin raise my hopes. I'd tried to write about it. Words wouldn't come. I would scribble a sentence and push aside the diary, the way an invalid can't eat. I tried to remember that pain passes.

I would lodge the call after Melissa left. While I went about the domestic chores, rinsing dishes and taking out the garbage, the phone message burned tantalisingly. Melissa was taking forever in the bathroom. I wanted to rush in and snatch her hair dryer away. I forced myself to make coffee and scan the headlines. I don't think one word registered. Finally, she wafted out, perfumed and smiling.

As soon as she was gone, I dialled the Sydney number. A cheerful young voice answered.

'I'm looking for Kelly Anderson.' I was prepared for disappointment.

'She's just leaving for TAFE. Can I say who's calling?'

'Just Sara.' I felt sick and shaky. I could hear the background noise of a youthful household.

'She's coming now.' There was a thump, a peal of laughter. A voice of a new timbre spoke. 'Hello? This is Kelly.'

'Kelly? There was a message on my answerphone. I'm Sara Carmody, from Armidale.'

The silence seemed to last for ever.

'Are you my birth mother?'

Tears filled my eyes. 'I had a baby girl adopted in 1977. I don't know what her adoptive parents called her. I named her Shannon. An agency contacted me about an inherited blood disorder. Does this ring any bells with you?'

She spoke eagerly and I felt a huge weight lift. 'Well yes. Bells are ringing!'

'Kelly, I'd really like to meet you. Would you be willing?'

'Sure. Well, if you don't mind coming to me. I've bunged up my leg on a motor cycle. I'm actually in plaster.'

'Of course I'll come. When, do you think?'

'I'm at TAFE. Since the accident they pay

for me to go by taxi. What about next weekend?'

'I'll make a booking at once. What's your address?' I wrote it down as she said, 'I have to go. My taxi's arrived. This is awesome! I can't believe it.' She was gone.

Alone, I let my emotions overpower me. Molly eyed me gravely, then settled near her food bowl, nose on her paws, prepared to wait out my peculiar human torrent of tears and joy. The rest of the morning passed in a kind of dream. I cancelled appointments, phoned the railways and ran a load of washing, all the while engaged in imaginary conversation with Kelly. The power of the link I felt with her amazed me. I'd only had to hear her voice and I was overwhelmed.

I had been unaware of time passing. When Melissa returned, I wasn't ready to share Kelly with anyone. The visit to Roz must have gone badly. Melissa was hardly through the door before her temper exploded.

'You won't believe this! I drove Roz to the hospital, sat in the waiting room with her for over an hour, took her to the shops, carried the groceries for her and drove her home again while she spent the whole time complaining that nobody does a thing for her. *What about me?* I said. *Huh! You've made your priorities clear!* she said. *If I didn't ring you, you wouldn't bother to come near me.*

She was too caught up in her story to notice my detachment. 'Why can't we choose our parents, Sara?'

'For the same reason we don't choose our children, I suppose.' I hadn't meant to sound abrupt

'I didn't mean — you know I'm really grateful for everything.'

That night, writing again in a feverish outpouring as though spilling out decades of suppressed longing, I turned to my diary.

Suddenly I am reconnected to that tiny baby they gave me to hold, on a proviso that I must not think of her as mine or yearn for what I could not keep. Now I can understand Melissa's underhand behaviour when she first came home. A drive to find her mother overruled everything. Roz was calling her as Kelly calls to me. I feel a basic instinct to go to her, and it's so primitive, so strong, it has a savage quality. No power on earth will prevent our meeting now.

Of course I love my stepdaughter. I remember the moment I first set eyes on her round, sunny face. So vulnerable

she looked in her worn-out sandals and crumpled dress! I could tell Paul was good with her and they were close; yet she was motherless and had lost an irreplaceable part of her world. I stepped in to that breach and conscientiously I tried to fill it with all the close observation, the thought and care at my disposal. Together we went shopping for her clothes, chose her toys and library books, went to the swimming pool together while Paul worked. I discovered the meals she liked to eat and explained the codes of life I hold as basic. At first I set out to be a good stepmother. It took time. Then one day I realised I loved this little girl.

But the blood bond has a different feel to it. Towards Kelly I feel a sense of self-sacrifice I'm not even sure is healthy. My own nature doesn't seem to count at all. I want to be anything she admires. I want to say whatever words she likes to hear. I want to perform whatever part she foists on me. I will give her anything. She only has to show me what she needs. I don't understand any of this. Is this a mother's role, that in service to her child she *will lose herself, abandon her own needs? Or is that a mother's self-indulgent projection, to forgive all, meet every demand, accept any fault? Is this a better form of love? It frightens me.*

Those words were written in the flow of new emotions. By the time I arrived in Sydney, I just felt apprehensive. On the trip down, rehearsed scraps of dialogue had run continually through my mind. Common sense told me not to expect too much. Kelly and I might meet and talk just once. I checked in to the hotel where I sat like a statue, staring at the phone. Kelly was out when I rang through. I left my number and a message. She called back within half an hour.

'Sara? Are you coming over now?'

I forgot about taking a shower and ordering dinner. 'Of course. As soon as I can find a taxi.'

The address she'd given was in Harris Street; not far from the central business district. I paid the driver and knocked on the battered front door. It swung open at once, as though Kelly had been waiting in the hall. In that first instant, gazing at her freckled, cheerful face, I saw the illusion of her father. He faded; there she was, my daughter; dark, frizzy curls, generous build, a plaster cast encasing her right leg from thigh to toe.

'You look so young!' were her first words. Perhaps she'd expected a Kmart frock and cardigan. I followed her into a large room with poster-covered walls and well-worn chairs and sofas. 'The others have gone out. Thought they'd give us some space.' She glanced around. 'Sorry about the mess.'

'That's OK. My daughter's room looks much the same.'

'You have a family?' She sounded uncertain and I realised that she was probably as nervous as I was.

'Melissa's my step daughter. She's nineteen. Her father and I divorced.'

She grinned. 'Life's a bitch!' She pointed to the cast. 'I'm riding pillion passenger, minding my own business, and this car runs a red light. Wham! Two operations so far, and more to come.'

'Did the thrombophilia cause problems?'

'Bled like a pig; transfusions, the works. But I'm OK. I guess I'm lucky.'

'Will the leg heal normally?'

'Will I have a limp? I might. They say I'll get compensation. Sit down? I could make a cup of tea.'

'Yes. Please.' I felt light-headed. I'd hardy eaten at lunchtime. I was glad of a few minutes to sit quietly, letting my world readjust. Although the tone of the meeting was warm, we were both avoiding the word 'adoption'. She must have questions.

I drank the tea and ate a slice of the cake obviously bought for the occasion.

'I want to thank you, Kelly.'

'Me? Why?'

'For agreeing to meet. For advising me about the blood problem . . . '

'The doctor said I should notify relatives.'

'You didn't owe me that. You didn't want contact. What changed your mind?'

'That was five years ago. And my adoptive mother would have been upset. She used to say, 'Let the past be the past.'

'Used to?'

'She died last year. Liver cancer.'

'I'm so sorry. And your father?'

'They split up when I was twelve. He travels. He does help out with my course fees.'

So the strangers who could give my baby so much more than I were just flawed human beings. My anger passed as quickly as it came. This was no time for bitterness. This wasn't hard. We were going to get along. My focus was on Kelly.

'What are you studying?'

'Commercial art. I'm good at drawing. Is that something you do?'

'I'm afraid not. No talent in that direction.'

'I wonder where it comes from? My birth father?'

It was only natural she would want to know about him. 'I didn't know him well. It was teenage curiosity. We weren't in love. I believe he joined the family trade as a butcher.'

'A butcher?' She laughed. 'That's a change. My adoptive father's a diplomat. We travelled a fair bit — Italy, America.'

'Italy! That's always been a dream of mine.'

'It was a good experience, I guess.'

'I'm puzzled by one thing, Kelly. How did the agency contact you? They only had your old address.'

'Since my Mum died, I've been wondering about you. Recently I re-registered with the agency.'

Tears sprang to my eyes. I stood up and went to put my arms around her; Kelly smiled the sweetest smile I'd ever seen.

19

Martin

I hadn't been alone with Annie since her birthday outing. I couldn't get her out of my mind. I kept trying to fit the broken pieces of our past into some whole but nothing would gel. We weren't carefree teenagers now. There was Ben, and there were children to consider. Annie had always been impulsive; certainly not one for regrets and self-analysis. That was my role. I'd let myself be led, knowing quite well I shouldn't have gone alone with her to the Metz Gorge, that place of such strong memory. Had Annie really loved me during all those years apart? I kept having flashbacks and hearing words that made no sense in the mouth of a married woman. *I always knew you'd come back, Martin.* And all those easy references to the past, as though in her mind it was just yesterday that we were students and lovers. I couldn't guess what she'd made of our last meeting. Had it seemed like a love tryst, or a compulsive return to our memories? When I thought about it and forced myself to overlook the emotions we'd both felt, I knew I'd compounded my dilemma over Bruce. I had no idea how to face Ben, who had plenty of other problems on his mind. I did consider putting an end to things by packing up and taking Adam back to Newcastle. But that would mean disrupting his schooling again. Living with him in such cramped quarters wasn't ideal for either of us. His mess annoyed me, as my nagging no doubt reacted on him. Otherwise I thought we were making progress. A little discomfort seemed a small price to pay for that. In any case the lease only had another two months to run. I decided to stick it out.

The rent was due on Saturdays. When I knocked on Sara's door, Molly barked; otherwise the house seemed deserted. Eventually Melissa came to the door, half-asleep.

'Did I wake you?' It was after ten.

She nodded. 'Sara's in Sydney. Mysterious business.'

'I didn't know.'

'I had a gig.' She yawned. 'God, I hate musicians' working hours! No wonder we all die young.'

I had to agree; the conditions of a muso's working life were far from what the doctor ordered. I'd seen the night out in many a dim, smoky, noisy dive. Then, it was all part of the adrenaline rush. I said so and Melissa shook her head.

'There's no adrenaline for me. Never did I think music could be such a drag.'

I felt sorry for her. When income replaces inspiration, something has to give.

'Could be time to make other plans?'

'Maybe. Should have finished my degree. At least I'd be qualified to teach. I've had enough of weddings and birthday parties.'

'You do sound depressed!' I was closer to the truth than I'd meant to be. Tears filled her eyes.

'I *am* depressed. I hate life!'

'What you need is a good walk in the fresh air.' I found myself adopting the fatherly tone I use when Adam needs direction. 'Open those sleepy eyes and get dressed. We're going for a walk with Molly.'

'It's freezing!' she grumbled.

'I'll be back in fifteen minutes.' I must have sounded stern enough. She managed a wan smile.

In his pyjamas, Adam was directing aliens through a space attack on the computer screen.

'Do I *have* to?' he complained when I told him to get dressed and join us on the walk.

His babyish whining could thoroughly irritate me at times. 'Yes you do. And don't leave those breakfast plates on the floor.'

With a final burst of ray gun fire, he slammed the programme into shutdown mode and stamped off to get dressed.

Swaying in the bitter wind, stripped poplars along the avenue were hazing over with faint greenery. Melissa hitched up the hood of her jacket and thrust her hands in her pockets. Adam maintained a surly distance at the rear. We stepped out briskly, Molly pulling like a mad thing until my arm ached in its socket. In the fields, young animals stood at the mercy of the elements. I felt compassion for the twin new-born lambs guzzling beside their mother. It was a wonder they could survive. The sight of them sent Molly into a barking frenzy and the ewe issued a disapproving glare and moved off. I tugged at the recalcitrant dog, feeling like one of those harassed parents whose toddler throws a tantrum on the supermarket floor.

Melissa relieved me of the leash and, with a few sharp orders and stern wrenches on the choker, managed to control her.

'You have to show her who's boss, Martin.'

'I'm more of a cat person actually.' I didn't much care for the passionate excesses of dogs. I remembered how a school friend's terrier had once snapped at my hand, drawing blood. I'd meant it no harm, and had

never forgotten the injustice. 'You know
. . . *Dogs have owners, cats have staff?*'

Melissa giggled. The wind had brought
colour to her cheeks and her eyes were bright.
She glanced back at Adam.

'What's up with him?'

'He'd prefer a different father.'

'Why? You're not that bad. Why do people
have children, Martin?'

'Good grief! I've really no idea. It's not
always planned.'

'Then it should be!'

I laughed. 'Life's full of shoulds and
random happenings.'

'That's what I feel like; a random
happening.'

'That's nonsense! Sara cares a great deal
for you.'

'What about my parents? Paul goes
running off like an adolescent. And here's
the latest with my mother. She's planning to
go gold prospecting in the bush with her
boyfriend.'

'That's so terrible?'

'Snakes and spiders and kangaroos hop-
ping round the yard? Come on!'

'Sounds adventurous to me.'

'I think it's childish.'

'Melissa, we parents don't get some
handout of almighty wisdom when our

children are born. We just muddle through, same as you.'

Withdrawing into herself, she said no more. I suppose we must blame someone when our lives seem empty. I used to think I'd be a different, happier man, given some other upbringing. But I suspect our natures fit us as snugly as our skins, and it is up to us to accommodate their intricacies.

'Let's go back?' I suggested. Violet-grey clouds were claiming the hills. On the way home I kept an eye out for the lambs but they weren't in sight. I supposed the ewe had found a sheltered spot. As drizzle changed to a steady downpour, we all ran the last few hundred metres and arrived home dripping wet, but somehow the better for our outing.

'If you're free, join us for dinner,' I called after Melissa as she made a dash for the porch. She blew me a childish kiss that touched my heart. The fatherly role had some compensation.

★   ★   ★

I'd forgotten Bruce was due for a guitar lesson later in the morning. Ben usually dropped the boy off but today I saw Annie coming up the driveway through the rain. She looked as though she had something on her mind. With the children in earshot, I hoped it wasn't to do with us. However, her first words were about Ben.

'Has he been to see you?'

'No. Come in out of the rain.'

Bruce ducked inside but Annie shook her head. 'Joanne's in the car. So Ben hasn't brought you up to date then?'

'I haven't seen him since last week. What's happened?'

'The Council knocked back his application. We had a good talk, Ben and I. He's gone north to look for work. There's nothing for him here.'

'He's already gone?'

'A few days ago. He meant to call in. It was all such a rush.'

'It seems very sudden.' I felt a little disappointed that Ben hadn't bothered to say goodbye. It must have been a hard decision for him; for all the family. 'How will you manage meanwhile?'

She looked exhausted. Her hair hung in bedraggled tails and there were dark rings under her eyes. 'It won't be for long. There's plenty going in the mines up that way.'

'And that's the plan? You'll all relocate?' A sense of loss hit me hard.

'Once Ben has found a place.'

'It seems a bit drastic. What about the

children's education?'

'Ben's been under a lot of pressure,' she said slowly. 'Something had to give.'

'Could this be a passing mood?' I spoke carefully. 'Did you really think things through?'

'We decided this together.'

'I heard just recently of a man who took off. He turned up a few weeks later, after doing some thinking.'

'I just told you, we decided this together!' She sounded angry, though she had the look of an abandoned woman. I wasn't prepared to debate Ben's state of mind though I believed that sometimes pressures could build until the proverbial straw did its damage.

'He hasn't had bad news recently?' I asked casually. I knew that, had Annie chosen to open her Pandora's Box, it held enough calamities to unhinge the sanest man.

'Actually, he seemed quite excited at the prospect of a new start. I'm not saying it's going to be easy for us. But in the long run we'll all benefit.' She glanced back at the car. 'I'm taking Joanne shopping. Will Bruce be alright here till lunchtime?'

'He's welcome. Adam could do with a mate. We'll have our lesson first.'

'Thanks.' Briefly she rested a cold hand on mine. 'I'll see you later.'

I watched her run down the drive, then turned to Bruce. 'So what do you make of all this?'

'They had a pretty big row the other night.' He shrugged then. 'Maybe Dad has gone to find work. I just wish he'd said goodbye. I came home from school and Mum said he'd left. Can I dry my guitar, Martin? The rain might stain the wood.'

I handed him a cloth. Perhaps the self-centredness of children is a blessing. Without it, the unpredictable adult world would destroy them.

We were eating pancakes when Annie returned. She sank onto the couch, nodding when I insisted she and Joanne stay for lunch. The responsibility for her family was fully on her shoulders now.

'Working tonight?'

She gave a weary nod. 'Yes. I have to be on deck at five. I'm worried about the children, Martin. I don't like the idea of leaving them alone.'

'I'm sure Bruce is old enough to man the ship.'

Annie was doubtful. 'I don't suppose you could bring Adam and stay the night?'

I was silent, thinking. I didn't feel I had the right to so easily stand in for Ben. And yet Annie was alone now. I couldn't see the harm

251

in offering a bit of help. When my son had first arrived here, I'd been glad enough when Sara stepped into the breach. And Annie had gone out of her way to make Adam welcome.

Part of me wanted to pack an overnight bag and go with her then and there. The watcher, my other self, was issuing warnings, loud and clear. *Be careful. Don't get involved. This is more than you can handle. Back off!*

'I can't, Annie. Melissa's coming to dinner. She's a nice kid and she's been a bit down. Perhaps Joanne and Bruce can stay over, if you can drop off sleeping bags.'

'Well, thanks. I'll bring them on my way to work.'

A deserted, lost expression on her face, Annie stood up and brushed down her jacket. 'Come on kids, we have to face the world alone now.'

I felt like a heel. At a time of crisis, I'd failed her once before and altered her life irrevocably, yet she'd forgiven me. My independence was a mean excuse, beside that history.

'I've changed my mind.' I stopped her as she prepared to step out into the bleak afternoon. 'I'll come. Go and make us both a cup of tea, why don't you? I'll pop over and explain things to Melissa. She won't mind, it was only a casual invite.'

Annie turned back. 'I'll go and make the tea,' was all she said. But, strained as she was, her blue eyes briefly sparkled like those of the girl I used to know.

⋆   ⋆   ⋆

I wasn't home much at all over the next few weeks. Although it felt strange, moving in on Ben's terrain, Annie and I settled easily into a team. Of course Ben's shadow was everywhere; miner's overalls, boots and shoes, old tools lying around the place. He'd clearly travelled light and hitchhiked north rather than risking the journey in his battered ute. It stood deserted in the yard. While Annie waited to hear from him, she kept up her job and ran the three children to and from their schools. I saw to child minding, cooked when she was out and helped out with domestic matters. I slept in the spare room and was careful to act as nothing but a family friend. The boys were both of an age to be well aware of undertones.

After a few more tense days, Annie's mood improved. She told me Ben's plan was to head on up to the Northern Territory where he planned to try the bauxite mines. She thought he might have phoned that day but she'd been in the garden and missed the call. The children weren't home and I'd gone back to my flat to pick up my mail and fill Sara in on what was happening. I hadn't seen her since her trip to Sydney. She asked me in. We sat drinking coffee, catching up on the interim news. I told her I was more or less staying out at Annie's while Ben found work.

'Do you want to wind up the lease, Martin?'

'No!' I was startled by the suggestion. 'Not at all. I'm certainly not moving in with the Marshall family. They'll be packing up and going themselves soon.'

'When they're ready to join Ben, you mean?'

Her tone made me wonder if she thought the story was a fabrication; that Annie and I had other plans. I hastened to put her right.

'Just let me know about the flat,' she said, as though preferring not to become involved. 'I won't hold you to the lease, if you change your mind. Now I'll tell you my news.'

She had located her daughter. Apparently the meeting had gone well; in fact, better than her wildest dreams.

'I'm genuinely happy to hear it.' I meant it. Sara was one of the nicer people I'd met in a lifetime with its fair share of disappointments. She was successful, but it hadn't gone to her head. She'd had her share of pain without becoming self-pitying. She'd raised a step-daughter admirably. Her virtues were endless, and it was strange I couldn't bring myself to care about her, except as a friend. Annie, on the other hand, wasn't in the category of 'nice'. She'd deceived her husband in several ways. She was possessive, faithless, and obsessive. Somehow her faults hardly mattered. She moved me. I couldn't explain it.

As we sat chatting, the farrier arrived. Sara went to bring one of the horses in to the stable. I watched her deft manner as she steadied the nervy animal, talking softly while the man tapped and filed back the hooves. A feeling of nostalgia moved me as I breathed in the horse's earthy scent oddly mingling with Sara's perfume. Beyond the doorway I could see past the post and rail enclosure to the paddock with its soft green grass and fallen, rusting drums. I would miss the tranquillity of this place, even as I knew a phase had closed and an unknown future was unfolding. Of course I would be happy for the Marshall family when they were reunited, but I would miss them. With Bruce, I was gradually feeling my way towards a relationship that wasn't just a debt to him and Annie. He was very bright. I thought he could probably succeed in almost any profession. Annie's proposal to remove him to some back-of-beyond school really troubled me. It went against everything she'd professed to believe in and I could only account for it as the compromise of a bewildered and perhaps desperate woman intent on holding her family together at any cost. In the back of my mind I was working out some other option for the boy. Perhaps he could stay with Adam and me during term time, and we'd manage somehow to keep the school fees going. It would be a way of paying the debt I'd so woefully failed to meet when he was born. A second chance. We'd see.

20

Sara

After meeting Kelly, I felt as though a great wave had swept over my existing life. I intended to live in Sydney next year. My daughter could use my support. Her adoptive family links were gone and she had to face surgery. Most of all, I wanted to spend time with her and get to know her.

Melissa and I had a good talk about all this. She was open to the idea of a move. She confessed her regret at giving up her studies and was keen to complete her degree at the Sydney Conservatorium. With Roz moving to the country somewhere in central Queensland, there was nothing to hold Melissa in Armidale.

Martin had also moved on. Although he kept up the rent on the flat, he was hardly ever there. In my opinion, Annie had sent Ben packing and moved Martin in so smoothly I doubted he understood what she was doing. He seemed convinced that Ben was preparing to move the family to the far north but I would believe that when I saw it. Martin was an intelligent man, but I thought Annie was manipulating him. Well, it wasn't my business. Her story could be true. But I'd seen the way she looked at him. I'd heard the way she talked down to Ben. She certainly saw me as a rival.

Funny, that. Martin and I were never really an item. We circled round each other in that wary way. When he was interested, I stepped back; and vice versa. Just something off-centre. At least we'd helped each other settle past issues. I'd found Kelly, and young Adam seemed a more normal boy. I may have helped but that was mainly to Martin's credit. He was trying hard. These poor children, caught in the middle of their parents' problems! Melissa was angry that Roz was moving, but that was the pattern of her life. I was glad she was going. Without her mother, Melissa could examine what she needed for herself.

It would be a simple matter to rent my home. What to do with Molly was my major headache. I couldn't see her tethered in a tiny Sydney courtyard. Even here, she was cooped up too much and lately had shown a side of her nature I'd rather forget. The other day she killed one of the chickens. I tried the old trick of tying the dead bird around her neck. All

258

day she lay in the kennel, looking doleful, the lumpy carcass dangling whenever she moved, but next day she was eyeing the coop again. I feared she'd learnt nothing from the exercise.

★ ★ ★

My premonition was right. I was cooking tea several days later when there was an aggressive knocking at my door. A red-faced fellow in farmer's sou'wester and boots confronted me. *Do you own that border collie in the yard?* He sounded furious and my heart sank, because Molly had managed to slip out the back door and take off earlier in the day. She came home subdued and panting. Her ingratiating mood made me suspicious. I knew she'd been up to no good and it seemed I had every reason to worry. She'd been at the lambs up the road. One was bitten around the legs and the other was in shock. Fortunately, the farmer had heard the growls and barks and the bleating of the ewe and had chased Molly off. *If I'd been carrying my gun, I'd have used it. There's only one thing to do with an animal that has the taste of blood, lady. You better get on and see to it, or I will.*

When he'd gone, I brought Molly inside

and examined her closely. Traces of dried blood marked her white chest hair. *Oh Molly!* I held her close and cried my heart out. Why did nature persist in keeping these instincts active in a domestic dog that doesn't know what hunger is? Something had wakened that dormant drive in her to kill. I couldn't trust her again.

When Melissa came home I told her what had happened. She was upset but not all that surprised. She thought Molly had been hyperactive lately. Keeping her indefinitely tied up would probably make her worse. I let her curl up on my bed that night because I knew it would be her last. I had no sleep, and cried on and off the whole night, while Molly drowsed and woke, eyeing me with puzzled looks of solicitude.

★   ★   ★

In the morning I couldn't eat a thing.

'You look terrible!' Melissa said when she came to fix breakfast.

'I'm taking Molly to be put down.'

Melissa stared at me in horror. 'You can't!'

'It has to be done.' I felt flat and cold now; the way I'd once felt, signing the adoption papers. 'Sometimes you have to make hard decisions, Melissa. That farmer will keep his word. He'll be back with a gun if he sets eyes on her again.'

'She just needs exercise!' Melissa pleaded.

'Molly's a working breed. She should never have been kept on a town property, chained up so much. She needs the freedom of the open spaces. We're not going to have that in Sydney. I've made up my mind. It has to be done.'

'Then I'm coming with you.' She left the table angry, her cereal untouched.

I rang the vet and made an appointment. I fed Molly a huge plate of chicken, which she wolfed as though it was Christmas. She drank two plates of milk and flopped on the tiles, bulging. I brushed her silky coat, fondled her ears and kissed her damp nose. I put on her collar and lead. She wagged her tail at the prospect of an outing and waddled to the door.

'Melissa, it's time,' I called. She came in to the kitchen, not looking at me, and snatched up the lead. All the way along the road to town she sat with Molly beside her on the back seat, holding her close, small sobs escaping her. I kept repeating in my mind, *It has to be done. It has to be done.* Yes. This was the feeling from long, long ago, seeing my baby lying on the clinical white bosom of the nurse who carried her away.

As I pulled up in the vet's parking area, I could see Molly rest her head down on Melissa's lap in a resigned way as though the scents in the air did not speak of good things ahead. Tears streaking her face, Melissa held her close. There was going to be a scene. Stubbornly I got out of the car and went to open the back door. As I took hold of the leash, Melissa gave a cry.

'No, Sara! Wait!'

'You should have stayed at home if you can't handle this,' I said roughly, for I had to get through the next half-hour with some kind of control. 'There's no other option.'

'But there is! Roz will take Molly. She'd never want her put down. She adores dogs and where she's going there's all the room in the world.'

'That's a pretty big ask.'

'I just know she'll say yes! Oh please, can we go and see her now?'

'When does she leave the caravan park?'

'Soon. Next week. We'd have to keep Molly under lock and key till then.'

I sat thinking. Melissa didn't say a word. Molly lay like a corpse, as though hoping I wouldn't notice she was in the car.

'Alright! It's worth a try. We'll take Molly back home and go and talk to Roz right away.'

＊　＊　＊

That's what we did. Back home, I rang the surgery and said I'd been delayed. Melissa and I forced down tea and toast and plastered make-up on our ravaged faces. Then I locked Molly in the house and we headed to the caravan park, which was a pleasant little community with its shop, its avenues of trees and cabins. Roz and her boyfriend were sitting under their awning, having a smoke, when we walked over.

'Pull up a pew!' Roz was surprised at our visit and I felt ashamed I'd never once bothered to call in and say hello. 'Bring out those folding chairs, Brett.'

Brett wore stretched track pants and a baggy jumper. He had a week-old growth of beard, a straggling ponytail, and pale blue eyes that blinked regularly as though keeping time to music. His cap was on backwards and he wore sneakers without socks. Melissa had exaggerated about the teeth. He was only missing a couple in the front; noticeable as he whipped out the chairs and gave us a welcoming grin.

Melissa wasn't interested in social niceties. 'Mum! You have to say yes. Will you have Sara's dog? You remember her, she jumped all over you at our place.'

'Honey, the caravan park doesn't permit dogs or I'd take her like a shot. Are you two going away for the weekend?'

'I mean, will you have Molly permanently, at the property? If you won't, we have to kill her.'

'Christ, what for, for heaven's sake?'

'She chased lambs.'

'She *attacked* lambs,' I corrected her. 'The farmer's going to shoot her unless we put her down.'

I thought Roz had better know what she was taking on.

Melissa began to sob. Roz stood up and put a firm arm around her daughter.

'The bastard. Well, it's fine by me. What d'you reckon, Brett?'

'Dogs have the nature the Lord gave 'em,' announced Brett in a slow and meditative voice. 'Can't be blamed for that.'

'That's the truth, Hon,' Roz agreed. 'They come from wolves, way back. You don't expect a wolf to stay quiet in a kennel, do you?'

Brett nodded. 'The open space is what they were born to. There's no problem with having your dog. My hut's nowhere near farm animals. Wild pig, 'roos, nothing she could take on.'

'Be company for me. Might get lonely, just

Brett and me under the big wide open sky.'

'And the moon and stars. Don't forget them,' Brett said warmly. Roz reached for his hand. The pair were obviously in the early stages of romance. And I was glad that Roz was setting off on some new path. The pain she would save me by taking Molly seemed to make up for the past.

Melissa was triumphant as we drove home. Her mother had finally risen to the occasion and given her what she'd asked for. There was even forgiveness for the toothless one.

'Brett's not such a bad bloke. It might be fun, living in the bush for a while.'

For a while. At least Molly had her reprieve. Surely that was all any of us could count on? It was time to drop my grievances regarding Roz. Even if the adventure was short-lived, it had renewed whatever it was she pursued to feel alive. Meanwhile, I would spend the last months of the year attending to the many details of moving. Packing, cleaning, property to lease, my business to farm out while I was away. I wouldn't do anything too radical yet. Armidale would be my bolt hole, if things in Sydney didn't work out.

★ ★ ★

265

A most surprising invitation arrived. Martin called in, I thought to pay the rent, but after those formalities he told me Annie's mother was turning sixty-five and there was to be a party in her honour. Would I go?

I must say I was staggered. Annie couldn't stand the sight of me! But all that was apparently set aside now that she and Martin were a couple hosting a convivial family do.

'Any word from Ben?' I asked.

'Annie says he's rung a few times. Things are progressing. He has a few job locations picked out.'

'But you haven't spoken to him yourself?' I made the query casually but Martin gave me an odd look.

'Not personally, no. I wasn't there at the time.' He seemed uneasy as he changed the subject. 'I might as well tell you, I'd like to wind up the lease if you agree.'

'Of course. You're not going back to Newcastle yet?'

He seemed surprised I knew. 'That's right. Adam's settled down. I'm reluctant to uproot him. And I like it here. I've applied for a couple of teaching jobs. We'll see.'

'When the Marshalls go, you won't be lonely?'

'Why would I be? One makes new friends.'

I was sure his ties must be deeper than he

admitted. Time would tell. 'You can use the flat rent-free until I go. I won't be looking for another tenant.'

'I'm pretty settled at Annie's. It helps her when she's working. I'm becoming quite domesticated.'

'I expect you are.'

★   ★   ★

I had promised to attend the birthday party at *Windsong*. Curiosity had the better of me. It was quite a peculiar set-up out there at the Marshalls — the father gone, Martin standing in, and no one asking questions. More than a month had passed since Ben ostensibly went off to find a job. Long enough, I thought. My own opinion was that he'd left for good. Either he'd walked out on his demoralising life or Annie had made him leave. It puzzled me that Martin believed her. She'd lied in the past. I didn't like Annie. And yet we had more in common than I cared to think. We'd both been young girls; pregnant, frightened and alone. We'd taken different roads out of our dilemma. Fate had given Kelly back to me. If Annie wanted Martin so badly, perhaps she was due some happiness too. Martin was no fool. He wouldn't have been with Annie against his will.

The party was underway when Melissa and I pulled up mid-afternoon. The house hadn't improved under Martin's occupancy. The spring grass grew as lushly as ever and rundown machinery stood around the yard. A small gathering, Annie's relations, I guessed, stood about chatting. An old man dozed; his wheelchair tucked into a sheltered corner of the garden. Annie, in a white cotton frock and sandals, looked summery as she introduced her mother. I handed Nina her gift of perfume. Like a little girl she tore off the wrapping and sprayed us all liberally, giving little cries of pleasure. She was a dynamo of exuberance, dressed in retro, hippie-looking clothes. Peace and love! She wore an air of relaxation and fun that invited friendship. I felt I could trust her, and spilled out the story of my own mother's sad situation.

'Now she's had a stroke, on top of the senility,' I explained and Nina nodded sympathetically. 'Last weekend I pushed her wheelchair out into the garden at the Home to show her freesias and irises. She used to love gardening. But I could tell the flowers didn't mean anything now.'

'It doesn't seem fair, does it?' Her voice was kindly.

'No. And I'm riddled with guilt. I'm moving to Sydney in the New Year.'

'Your mother has lived her life. Now you must live yours. Don't wait for the future. Look at poor Doug. All the things he was going to do when he retired . . . '

'It must be very hard on you.' I couldn't imagine myself at my mother's beck and call, day in, day out.

'You do what's needed.' She gave a brisk shrug and the string of little bells at her neckline jiggled. 'Make the best of every day. Martin and Annie seem happy, don't they? Of course I knew Martin long ago. So talented. Just a slip of a fellow, always looked underfed. He loved my home-baked cakes! Isn't it kind of them to put on this party for me? It's good to see them so settled. A happy home makes such a difference.'

'You'll miss your daughter and the children when they join Ben.' I was fishing. An expression of reserve settled on Nina's face.

'I certainly will. Whenever that happens.'

'Soon, surely? There's plenty of work up north.'

'You could be right there. Excuse me, Sara. The birthday girl must circulate!'

She glided away as though dancing to a rhythm only she could hear. In the chair, her husband began to snore.

Martin was handing a tray of drinks around. Melissa had joined the young people and Adam was off playing makeshift rounders with Bruce and two other boys. Apart from Annie, I knew nobody else. I passed her, standing with an older man, some relative, who was telling her a joke as I went by. Annie's quick peal of laughter stayed in my ears as I walked towards the back yard, where Ben's old ute still stood. Convolvulus was taking over, twining around its wheels. Atop its bent aerial, I saw one glorious violet-blue flower, already fading as the afternoon closed in.

21

Martin

I'd been with Annie and the children for several months. With police enquiries under-way, the Christmas period was unpleasant for all of us. Annie insisted it was all a storm in a teacup. She was still sure that Ben would show up in his own good time. But his brother called in and said enough time had passed; a man doesn't just vanish into thin air. None of us wanted to think an accident had befallen Ben on his long journey north, though a couple of unrelated news items presented grisly options. The police obviously took that possibility seriously. We were all interviewed; Annie, myself, even the children. The fact that I was living at the Marshalls aroused their interest. What was my relation-ship with the Marshall family? With Annie in particular? At that time I was still maintaining my distance in the spare room, and could truthfully say there was nothing between us. I was no more than an old friend and had been hoping to hear from Ben and then see the family off when they went to join him. Other questions made me equally uneasy. Had Ben seemed depressed or spoken of leaving home? True, I'd wondered if Ben had suffered amnesia or a nervous breakdown. The police seemed equally ready to consider mugging, suicide or even murder. They visited the house on a number of occasions and went over his ute with a fine toothcomb. Finally they listed him as a missing person, advising Annie that they would meanwhile pursue all avenues of enquiry. I must say we were both relieved when these cross-examinations stopped.

For a short while longer, Annie maintained her story that Ben left because he had no work and would not be kept by his wife. She insisted he would establish himself and then contact the family. When little Joanne put on her pensive look and asked *When's my daddy coming home?* Annie would scoop her up. Opening the map of the Northern Territory, she would point to some imaginary mine site and cuddle her daughter close, promising, *Soon, my darling, very soon. Daddy's finding work. Then we'll all be together in a nice house with lots of toys.* That seemed to mollify the child. She would lean against her mother's breast for a moment, then slip down and run off to play.

As January drew to an end, the household

spoke less and less often about Ben. My relationship with Annie was changing, fuelled by the everyday intimacies of life together and the special attentions Annie showered on me. As I stood in as acting father to the children, the divisions blurred. Hers, mine, ours — somehow paternal proof no longer seemed to be the criterion. I kept thinking of Hardy's viewpoint, expressed through Jude. The young are our collective responsibility, each child in need of parental care and supervision on the path to healthy adulthood. It was a pleasure to see Adam and Bruce settle in, like brothers to each other. The boys busied themselves with normal teenage interests. My heart lifted to hear their laughter as they wrestled and fooled about. There were no more chapters to Bruce's novel, and Adam responded to Annie's mothering — one skill she excelled in.

For some time I had been well aware that Annie wanted to move me from the spare bed to her own. I had to be sure she'd told me the truth about Ben's leaving. One evening after the children had gone to bed, I asked her exactly how they'd parted. For a moment she was quiet, as though remembering.

'You know the facts,' she reminded me. 'He went to find work.'

'Annie, I think it's strange that Ben hasn't

273

written to the children. He was devoted to them.'

'Ben write letters? It's not his way.' She gave a shrug.

'Then he would telephone in the evening, when he could speak to them,' I persisted. 'Be honest, please. You said he'd phoned you. Was that true?'

She didn't speak but shook her head.

'Annie! Why lie about it? What did Ben know about us? About Bruce? Did you tell him the truth? We'll never be free, unless you tell me.'

'Alright. I told him everything.'

I'd known as much. She spoke calmly, as though the truth erases responsibility for the pain we cause. I didn't want to imagine how Ben must have felt. How could Annie, who is the soul of kind-heartedness, dispense such devastating information?

'But why tell him now, after all this time!' Nobody could bear such cold truth. *Kindness and lies* — the salve of human bonds; the phrase from Graham Greene drifted into my mind. Perhaps I'd stored it, to justify some of my own past concealments in relationships.

'I had to,' was all she said. There were tears in her eyes.

★ ★ ★

For days I withdrew into myself, thinking about all this in the midst of family pandemonium. A man could only bear so much humiliation. Ben was worn down by circumstance. He carried the burdens of inferiority — of lack of education, past mistakes and loss of employment. Earning had fallen on his wife's shoulders; to him, a shameful situation to bear. And then to learn she wanted another man, and always had, and that he was Bruce's father! Flight would have been a logical next move for him. How else could the Marshalls' story end? And where did that leave me? We both knew Ben wasn't coming back.

We may think we go in search of pleasure and self-satisfaction but amid my unsettling thoughts I found my only peace in duty. Outwardly the children held our routines in place. They occupied a good part of our joint time and energy. Annie was more used to this than I was. Privacy doesn't go with family life. I realised how selfishly much of my life had been lived.

My delays and doubts were getting on Annie's nerves.

'I can hardly believe Ben would abandon you all,' I insisted, speaking my repetitive thoughts aloud. That Ben had simply left his family somehow shocked me. Annie had already lied to me. I was wondering what other misfortunes might account for Ben's absence.

'You don't know Ben. When he made up his mind, that was that.' She sounded abrupt.

True enough. We weren't close friends. We'd only met a dozen times, and then in a family context. I liked him and felt vaguely indignant on his behalf, as one would feel for any man who trudges from door to door, seeking work and meeting with rejection. I knew I was in the privileged bracket and was about to take up a teaching position locally.

While Annie lavished small attentions and smiles upon me, she hardly spoke of Ben at all. He may as well have been a visitor in her life. Perhaps the strain of the past had sapped her feelings for him. Did they count for nothing, all those years shared in homemaking and having children, making plans, working side by side, sharing the small and large hopes of life? Ben had apparently deserted Annie. Why did she show no sign of outrage, anger, hurt? When Carol left me, I was miserable for quite a time.

'Don't think about him,' she murmured. 'He's a survivor. Wherever he is, he'll be alright.'

But I couldn't dismiss him. I was living in his shoes, had taken over his wife's love and his children's upbringing. Often I found myself in dialogue with his image, confessing my weak past and the trail of mistakes I'd left behind me. Mentally I told Ben that none of this was planned. I never meant to cause trouble. I hadn't come looking for some long-lost fantasy of love. That was Annie's obsession, not my own. She hid the truth of Bruce from both of us. Mentally I begged him to see my intentions now as honourable. I promised that, as long as he was absent on whatever quest drove him, I would act in good faith here. Should he ever return and convince Annie otherwise, I would quietly go away. We talked in spirit, late into my sleepless nights.

These weeks were hard. *Where is my daddy?* pleaded Joanne, curled in a chair, thumb in mouth; a habit Annie said the child had abandoned years ago. Unlike her mother I could not think of glib things to say. *He's gone away for a while*, I answered and her lip quivered. *Why?* Her voice had such a plaintive note!

Then I would think of the many children, perhaps the majority in these days of splintered partnerships, who must ask that same question in that same bewildered way. I began to review my dislike of the grim endurance of those long, embattled marriages common in the past. My parents died relatively young, within a year of each other. My mother's heart, or hope, gave out. When she was gone, Dad drank himself into oblivion. I had no understanding of the painful knots that had bound them. They hadn't shared much happiness but they were twin beacons I could rely on.

It was around this time that Annie's father was struck by a succession of further strokes. It seemed Nina had hardly notified us that Douglas was in hospital before the news came that he was dying. I stayed home with Adam and Joanne while Bruce and Annie went to say their goodbyes. They returned late, saying Nina had chosen to stay on by his bedside.

'He won't last the night.' Annie sounded weary. However estranged we may feel from our parents, their death diminishes us.

★   ★   ★

At the funeral Nina wept. Annie didn't shed a tear, hiding whatever she was feeling. Afterwards Nina came home with us. She sat, food and drink forgotten, looking fragile in her black outfit. The corner of the veranda seemed conspicuously empty as though Douglas, so inert in life, had become more present through his death.

278

'Mum's taking it hard.' Annie had drawn me aside, wondering if we could offer the spare room to Nina if she preferred to stay. I agreed, offering to sleep on the sofa; still in no-man's-land. If I ended up in Annie's bed it would be by choice, not as a displaced houseguest!

Knowing what I did about Nina, I expected her, after a decent interval of mourning, to welcome the release from the burden of her husband's care. Nina did stay the night and I did sleep on the sofa. The shift, slight as it was, jolted the paralysing block I felt. I moved to Annie's room soon after, expecting awkward repercussions with the children. Surprisingly little was said or implied. Perhaps children are wiser in the world than we know. In any case, presumably they didn't object to signs of love about the house.

Well, Annie finds love so simple! Her joy bubbled over in laughs and smiles and small gestures of service to her children and to me. She set down a meal or ironed a shirt as though privileged. Just as summer deepened and she shed the weight and bulk of winter garments, so her mood lightened. She seemed young and happy again, as though a long hard endurance test had ended to her credit.

★ ★ ★

There was to be no going back for me. My days were full and busy with all the practical matters of work and family life. I did leave my unit rented for the present, but cut all other ties with Newcastle. Seiko, my little cat, was transported and ensconced with the rest of Annie's menagerie and seemed pleased enough with the change of scenery. I had my goods brought up to Armidale. My leather couch and glass-topped table sat strangely with Annie's motley furniture. I knew family wear and tear would soon knock them into more accommodating shapes. My taste would have suited Sara's calm elegance much better. There was a time when I'd thought the same thing about Sara and myself. I became very fond of Sara. Who knows, without Annie, we might have come to some agreement. At least we managed to remain friends, promising to keep in touch once she moved to Sydney. And, being Sara, she kept her word. From time to time an email would come through on Bruce's computer. He liked to tease his mother, brandishing it in such a way she couldn't help but comment on my 'girl-friend'. In fact, Annie had no concept of such a simple thing as friendship between man and woman. All or nothing, Annie's motto.

Most of our time was taken up with the trivia of children's sandals, the dog's fleas, sausages smoking on the barbecue, mislaid keys, trips to the supermarket with the attendant eccentricities of Annie's old car. Finally I conceded we must buy something more reliable. I had my licence back and we were making regular Sunday excursions to explore the various scenic drives around the area. On the way out of town we would pass Sara's house; now tenanted, Molly and the horses gone, an unfamiliar red Holden in the driveway. We would picnic, then wander marked trails and tracks leading in to surprising waterfalls, deep brownish pools, bright streams bubbling amid the river stones. Such places reduced us to silence. Even the children would grow subdued in the face of evolution's patient work. Sometimes clothed in greenery, sometimes nothing else but rock, mountains reared up and cliffs fell away to unimaginable depths. There was a vastness and a peace there.

Standing by Annie, gazing at these heights and precipices, I would glance at her clear, untroubled brow and Ben would come unbidden to my mind. A suspicion would return, that somehow she had engineered his disappearance. I knew it was nonsense. Such an act would be not only morally evil but also, for Annie, physically impossible. Ben was a big, burly fellow, and Annie is a small woman. I was ashamed of those fantasies. I knew I had to accommodate, accept some mystery.

Nina sometimes joined us for these outings. Her affair seemed to have dropped away, almost as though Douglas was an essential factor in the equation.

'Are you lonely?' I asked her recently. Though Douglas could hardly have been good company, Nina's spirit seemed diminished. 'Do you miss your husband?'

'Of course. Forty years of my life has gone.' She sounded irritable.

'I hope you will forgive my saying this . . . ' I meant to cheer her up. 'Your life with him wasn't altogether happy, was it?'

'What's happiness got to do with it?'

She sat stubbornly silent. Wasn't the pursuit of happiness a *sine qua non* for everyone? Perhaps she meant that, good or bad, it was experience that creates us. If we could change the past, with all its pains and disappointment, we would lose what we have become.

'And what about you, Martin?' She turned the question back on me. 'Are you happy?'

I laughed at her dry tone. 'I would say so.' *Do you love Annie?* she was asking. I knew she picked up on the caution that crept in to my voice. Just a few nights before, Annie had hugged me playfully and demanded, like a child, 'Tell me you love me!'

I wanted to say the words. I caressed her hair, kissed her gently. She waited. I thought of Ben. Annie's wondering look fortunately passed as quickly as it came. We live with the natures we are born with. I knew love justified all, in Annie's book. She'd made it her calling and her quest. I stood back. In my dreams a body went hurtling through space, catching on outcrops and branches as it descended to some deeply-wooded grave. Oh, I reminded myself these were inventions. Ben had disappeared, as people sometimes do. But I lived with doubt and I was silent.

★   ★   ★

It was my turn to cook and supervise while Annie went off to her waitressing. I was reading Joanne her bedtime story when the phone rang. I heard Bruce speak, and felt Joanne grasp my hand.

'No, stay here. Finish my story, Martin!'

So I did, then tucked her up and went out to the living room. Bruce was standing at the window, his back to me.

'Who was on the phone?' I'd been expecting to settle the start date for my new job.

'Dad.'

I felt an extraordinary burden lift from my shoulders when I heard that muffled word. Ben was alive and well.

'He's not coming back. He said he just wanted to tell me himself. He wouldn't talk much. He just said it's for the best and when I'm older, I'll understand. But I won't!'

'I'm so sorry, mate. At least we know now that your father hasn't come to any harm.'

Suddenly Bruce was crying bitterly, ashamedly; dashing at his tears with an angry hand. '*He* might be alright. What about us now?'

As I saw his lost expression I felt some hard knot dissolve. I didn't want to fend off this emotion, because I empathised with him. For a moment I too was just a child in pain, and had done nothing to deserve it. I went to him and awkwardly put my arm around him.

'Now listen to me. I'm not your first choice, but I do promise you one thing. I won't leave. I will do my best to take care of all of you.'

My urgent words had nothing to do with my likely parentage; that issue Annie and I had decided we would keep quiet about until the time seemed right. No, I was desperately sorry for Bruce and wanted him to know I wasn't mouthing idle words. He gulped, pulled himself together and stepped away.

'Thanks,' was all he said. 'I'd better get on with my homework now.'

'Need a hand?'

'Me the genius? Not likely.' He managed a wan smile. 'By the way, Dad gave me a message for Joanne. He loves her. All that.' He sounded totally confused.

'Will that keep till the morning? She's settled for the night.' I preferred that Annie be at home to handle whatever reactions the little girl might show. Bruce nodded, then went off to his room and shut the door. I sat staring at the silent phone. Ben had made his choice and all I could do now was make my own. My course was quite clear to me. The loss of a father or a mother is a terrible blow, but children have the gift of living in the present. And Annie and I would be here with them, doing our best to aid the healing.

I told Annie when she came home from work. At first she was silent. Then some dam broke and I saw her calm control in the recent months had been some sort of defence. At last she wiped her eyes dry and sat huddled and vulnerable, as though fearing I would now leave too.

'For what it's worth, I'm here,' I said.

'Are you only staying for the children?'

'No, Annie. Partly for them.'

'Do you love me, then?'

Her voice was husky, brusque. There it was again; the question I had dreaded all my life and done everything to avoid. Why had I always heard it as a demand? I knew I would be miserable for the rest of my days if I walked away from Annie and the children now. So I took her in my arms. 'Yes, I love you.' And we held each other close.

In bed, we lay together after the intimacies of sex were done with. I stroked her back and murmured the affections she was waiting to hear until, curled up beside me, she fell asleep. Soon my arm began to cramp. I shifted and lay quietly, thinking about Ben. An owl hooted. Crickets chirped. Some witty night bird set off a stream of chirrups and cackles. I must have drowsed then. Later, in dawn light, I felt Annie reach out and take my hand. In rooms around us, the children were waking and the morning routines would soon begin.

We do hope that you have enjoyed reading this large print book.

Did you know that all of our titles are available for purchase?

We publish a wide range of high quality large print books including:
Romances, Mysteries, Classics
General Fiction
Non Fiction and Westerns

Special interest titles available in large print are:
The Little Oxford Dictionary
Music Book
Song Book
Hymn Book
Service Book

Also available from us courtesy of Oxford University Press:
Young Readers' Dictionary
(large print edition)
Young Readers' Thesaurus
(large print edition)

For further information or a free brochure, please contact us at:
Ulverscroft Large Print Books Ltd.,
The Green, Bradgate Road, Anstey,
Leicester, LE7 7FU, England.
Tel: (00 44) 0116 236 4325
Fax: (00 44) 0116 234 0205

Other titles published by
The House of Ulverscroft:

LEAVING GAZA

Margaret Sutherland

Ruth, an Israeli writer who grew up amid gunfire and grenade, startles the genteel artistic world of Barbara and Heath Barnes. Barbara still lives and paints in her Australian hometown. Ruth's arrival coincides with Barbie's declaration of war on a life she now sees as subservient and controlled. Heath misunderstands Barbara and Ruth is drawn in to fill the growing rift. But following a crisis, Barbara's future lies in ruins. Peace is a hard-won trophy — and, like her admired early Australian women painters, she sets out on the road to freedom and the right to become herself.